THE O'MALLEY & SWIFT CRIME THRILLERS

Corn Dolls
Foxton Girls
We All Fall Down
The House of Secrets
The Uninvited Guest
Deadly Games
One Last Breath

DEADLY GAMES

Copyright © 2023 by K.T. Galloway

Published worldwide by A.W.E. Publishing.

This edition published in 2023

Cover design by Kate Smith

Edited by GS & LW

www.ktgallowaybooks.com

DEADLY GAMES

AN O'MALLEY & SWIFT NOVEL
BOOK 6

K.T. GALLOWAY

To every single reader of the O'Malley & Swift series... thank you!

THE SIXTH INSTALMENT IN THE BESTSELLING O'MALLEY AND SWIFT CRIME THRILLER SERIES!

Tick, tick, tick... BOOM.

When Annie O'Malley and DI Joe Swift are called to the local park to investigate reports of vandalism, they begin one of the most harrowing cases of their career.

The vandal is a scared young woman with a bomb strapped to her chest and a list of games she must play.

As the games get more gruesome, the young woman has a choice to make; kill or be killed.

O'Malley, Swift, Tink, and Page find themselves racing against time to uncover who is behind the games before the bomb detonates.

But it soon becomes clear that the games-master is a thrill seeker and he's out to have fun, no matter how deadly the consequences.

Perfect for fans of LJ Ross, Alex Smith, Elly Griffiths, and Rachel McLean. O'Malley and Swift return in a thrilling instalment that will keep you hooked from the first page.

MAILING LIST

Thank you for reading DEADLY GAMES
(O'Malley & Swift Book Six)

While you're here, why not sign-up to my reader's club where you be the first to hear my news, enter competitions, and read exclusive content:

<u>Join KT Galloway's Reader Club</u>

A NOTE FROM KT

Well, here we are at book six! Can you believe it?

I loved writing Deadly Games, it was a romp. Full of fun and silliness as well as the usual exciting crimes to solve.

As per all of my other books, Deadly Games is set in Norfolk, but any streets/places/people and events are all fictitious.

So without further ado, buckle up and let's get going...

PROLOGUE

JESSICA FRAMPTON PULLED THE COURT DOORS CLOSED behind her and made her way out into the dark March evening. The frost had already settled on the cobbles, casting them as miniature icebergs in a sea of slush. She stepped carefully across the ornate pathway and onto the lawns in front of the magistrates' court where she was less likely to slip up and break an ankle on the way to her car.

It was quiet; Jessica had worked late again, staying behind after the judge had heard her prosecution statement and listened to the plea of the defence. There was no way she'd be losing this case; it had a stack of solid evidence and a handful of reliable witnesses to boot. The jury had been hooked on her every word during the closing speech, their nods and sympathetic eyes had spurred her on. With her razor-sharp suit, perfect blunt fringe, and cat-like green eyes, her spiked heels had clacked across the wooden floor of the court room and her arms had gesticulated wildly. Jessica had to remind herself to reel it in a bit. This wasn't an America drama. But it had been a hard slog to get where she was, especially from a council estate background, with a run of scholarships won with grit and determination and a hard-earned pupillage with the Crown Prosecution Service, Jessica loved her job and when she was on a roll, that love shone out of every pore.

It must have rained while court had been in process, it hung in the air, blunting the edges of the icy cold, though it didn't take long for the tips of Jessica's fingers to numb. She rubbed her hands together and tucked them into the pockets of her duffle coat. The grass underfoot was spongy, with each step her heels sunk a little into the mud, slowing her down. Still, slow and steady was better than slipping on the wet cobbles. Somewhere in the distance a siren rang out, traffic lights beeped, a man coughed. Protected by the wall surrounding the courts, Jessica felt like she was in a bubble and, hearing the noises of a normal evening start to filter in, she wasn't sure she wanted to be deposited back into real life. She'd get to the car, blast out Taylor Swift, even if, at thirty, she was too old for it according to her ex-husband (one of the many reasons he was an ex), and the twenty-minute drive home would be a therapeutic song session to blast away the stresses of the trial. Her son, Oliver, was with his dad this evening, so Jessica had a large glass of wine with her name on it as a treat for when she got in. She missed him like crazy, but though trials were the most exciting part of her job, they were also the most draining. And this one had been no exception. Looking after a happy go lucky three-year-old was not always possible when she had nothing left to give. It made her feel like a bad mother that she was so focussed on her work and the not-so-subtle digs from her ex didn't help (reason number two he was an ex), but her clients needed her too. They needed a voice.

Sometimes Jessica felt sorry for the people she was charged to prosecute; the women beaten to breaking point by angry, entitled partners, the desperate addict forced into armed robbery to simply meet their basic needs, they were a product of a broken system not a broken person. But not this time. This trial was an open and shut case of jealousy and revenge. Her client had been a young woman, not too unlike herself. Forced entry witnessed by the neighbours. Screams heard by passers-by. Known drug dealer, Henry Chance, covered in blood with the weapon in his hands when he was arrested and had confessed before he'd even reached the police vehicle. Unable to accept that this young woman with her whole life ahead of her had chosen to be with another man, he'd flipped and stabbed her, so she no longer had that choice. A moment of madness that his defence were trying to use to their advantage.

But there was another death on this man's hands that was helping to swing the minority in the jury who were complacent about a dead woman. A drug deal gone wrong; a young man no longer able to celebrate his birthday because of a dodgy batch of speed. This was a case that Jessica would be sure to win. If winning was the right word when there were two dead people involved.

She sighed and pulled her shoulders together, hunching her coat around her neck. The wind was picking up now, chasing away any clouds in the sky and the blanket of warmth they offered. Her backpack was heavy, laden with papers she had meticulously drawn up over the course of the last few weeks. A ritual of shredding lay ahead of her, kindling for her wood burner, but only once the jury had made their decision. It was out of her hands now, and more than anything, Jessica wanted to go and wash her hair of the itch that her peruke caused. Horsehair and hemp weren't the kindest of materials for a blunt fringe and bob, even if it did look pretty cool. She pulled a hand from her pocket and ran warmed fingers through her dark black hair, feeling the grease weighing it down, and grimacing.

The pools of orange light from the court lanterns only reached to the edge of the court gardens. As Jessica stepped off the grass and onto the pavement by the gates, she could see the entrance to the car park. She hated this bit. The few meters of darkness between her work and her Audi E-Tron, a well-earned gift to herself on her first anniversary of pupillage. The only thing she'd splashed out on, frivolous perhaps, as a single mum, but Jessica knew she deserved a treat. Walking out past the gates, she checked the road, looking left and right even though she'd be able to hear a car if it was driving towards her. The road was clear, but in the shadows of the alleyways that littered the old streets, Jessica was sure she saw movement. A flicker. Perhaps it was a cat. Or a solar bulb struggling from the limited March charge.

A shudder worked its way up Jessica's arms, nestling in the base of her neck like an insect, tickling her scalp. She shook it out, glancing again at the alleyway. There was nothing there now. It was empty except for the flutter of an empty packet of crisps. She was tired, and a little strung out from the descriptions of the attack she'd just given to the members of the jury. It was probably her imagination. Why would someone be hiding behind the stone wall? No, she was being daft. Chewing at the inside of her cheek, Jessica pulled her backpack higher on her shoulders, ducked her chin down into her collar, and stepped out into the road.

"Watch out!" A cyclist swerved around her as she stumbled back a step, catching her heel on the curb, and almost dropping onto her backside to the damp ground.

"I'm so sorry," she called after him, catching her balance, but the bike was already too far away to hear her apologies.

Her heart was thumping in her chest, pounding the blood to her ears. Though they were almost numb with the cold, Jessica's hands felt clammy with sweat. Something was off, she could feel it in her bones. She was used to paying attention to her gut instincts, using them on more than one occasion to figure out the real cause of a suspicious death or the frame of mind of the accused, so Jessica knew she should listen to it now but at the same time, the very idea something was wrong seemed totally nonsensical. It wasn't even that late. It was Friday.

This is what happens when you work too hard, Jess. She wiped her hands down her coat and hoiked up her backpack once again.

With the noise of the bag rubbing against her coat and the blood still furiously pulsing in her head, the sound of the coughing could have been imagined. Jessica held her breath, straining to hear past the noises of her own body; and there it was again. A cough. Nothing sinister about that, it was probably another court worker, or someone making their way back from an early evening pint in the city centre. But the way it cut through the frost made the acid in Jessica's stomach wash over itself with a sickening jolt of dizziness. Checking the coast was clear, she stepped out into the road and made her way quickly across it to the carpark entrance at the other side. Her body was tense, she could feel it in the way her coat rubbed along her ears and her hips cried out at her to stretch her steps.

The smell of urine hit the back of Jessica's throat as she pushed open the door to the multi-story and relief flooded through her at the brightness of the foyer and the sight of her car past the concrete half-wall. There were a couple of court appointed spaces on the ground floor of the multi-story, to make up for the lack of parking on site. Jessica paid quickly for her ticket, sliding her bank card from her purse, and tapping it against the machine. Her fingers fumbled, not able to get purchase on the ticket as it was spewed back at her from the slot, her bank card and purse wobbled in her other hand, the card sliding over the leather of the purse and threatening to drop to the urine-soaked floor. She gripped on tightly, her finger-tips white with the force of keeping her card from falling, and snatched her ticket from the machine.

Clumsily, Jessica tucked the ticket between her dry lips and shoved her hand into her coat pocket, pushing down her purse without doing it up first. She felt the coins drop one by one onto the lining, but she hurried on towards her car, not wanting to stop to sort it out. She was nearly there. Nearly at her car, and her promise of a glass of wine was ever closer.

Overhead, the lights flickered on, one by one, casting long shadows from the concrete pillars across the tarmac. Jessica's heels clattered loudly, though the wind whistling through the open sides of the carpark was almost enough to drown them out. Cutting across the floor, she lurched forwards to the Audi and grabbed the handle, pulling the door unlocked and throwing herself towards the driver's seat. The sweet smell of candy floss rose like a comfort blanket from the Jelly Belly hanging from the rear view mirror reminding her that life wasn't always angry men with the opportunity to harm. But before Jessica could sink into the seats and pull the door shut behind her, she felt something tugging at her backpack. Her legs turned to jelly, knees folding and hitting the side of the seat with a thud. Wincing with pain, she turned, shoving her shoulders up to try and release her bag from her arms, not wanting to turn and see what had a hold of it.

"You look in a bit of a pickle there, you're hooked on your door, can I offer you a hand?" The voice was calm, recognisable, but Jessica couldn't quite place it.

Laughing a little at how she must look, knock-kneed and half folded into her car, she bent her head around to peer under her armpit at her saviour. And in doing so she saw it coming. A hypodermic, the needle as long as a horse tranquilliser, a black gloved hand, and a sharp pain in her thigh. The only thing going through Jessica's head as she fell into a deep sleep was the image of her son, his bright blue eyes and his rosy, red cheeks, how she may never bury her head into his hair and sniff him again. And how unfair that would be.

ONE

WRITING ON THE WALL

FRIDAY 9pm

"GRAB A VOL-AU-VENT AND FOLLOW ME." ANNIE O'Malley nodded in the direction of a platter of neatly arranged puff pastry casings with prawns poking out the top, and thumbed towards the door.

Not waiting for DI Joe Swift, she took off out of the open plan office and headed down the corridor, passing officers she didn't recognise because they looked like different people in their party outfits. Tinny radio music followed her, its high-pitched tones harmonised by the low rumble of the chatter of staff all merry on a couple of glasses of warm wine.

Annie poked a head around a half open door and beckoned behind her for Swift to follow.

"In here," she said, entering the nicest of the four incident rooms the police station had to offer. "Quick."

The door swung shut behind her, blocking the noise from the staff party. Annie took a few deep breaths of clear air, the smell of perfume and hot food not permeating through the door. Swift pushed into the room only moments later, a platter of food in one hand, a bottle of wine in the other, two plastic tumblers wobbled around over the screw top.

Annie laughed. "I said grab *one*, not the whole plate."

"I didn't know how long you were planning on keeping me away from the festivities," Swift replied, putting the platter and wine down on the table in the middle of the room. "I couldn't risk starving to death because of your resistance to mingle."

He twisted the top off the wine and carefully poured it into the two tumblers. Annie took one and helped herself to a puff pastry prawn.

"You'd rather be out there listening to Robins over-accentuate every word in an attempt to seem sober?" Annie pulled out a chair and sank into the plastic.

Robins was their DCI, and she'd had Annie running around all day chasing her tail for a piece of evidence from their last case that had gone AWOL from the evidence cupboard. She'd eventually found it in the wrong box, but not before blisters had appeared on her heels. Annie wasn't the most party-loving person at the best of times, and this Friday evening's gathering to wave off one of the senior officers into retirement made her feel like an imposter.

Annie O'Malley had started her adult life in the police force, a job which ended six months after it started due to personal circumstances that she was still talking through with her therapist. She'd gone on to train as a psychotherapist working in the probation team, a job she was good at that kept her on the periphery of the law. When Swift had brought her onto the case of a missing child, Annie had fallen hard and fast for the profiling work. She worked another couple of cases before she was formally recruited to the Major Crime Unit, a team made up of four people, herself included. DI Joe Swift, DS Tink Lock, and DC Tom Page. They were her family now, but still Annie often felt like she walked into conversations in the station that ended abruptly in her presence. *She jumped the recruitment stage. She was never a bobby on the streets. Who's she sleeping with to get that quick promotion?*

Truth be told, Annie didn't feel like opening up to these gossipers and letting them know she *did* complete her police training, most of it anyway. If she did that, she'd have to tell them why she left, and there were only so many times she could repeat her life story; how her dad upped and left when she was young, taking her baby sister with him to join a cult.

How her mum had smothered her with a weird kind of standoffish protection. How she had no idea what happened to her dad or sister; until now.

"Penny for your thoughts?" Swift waved a hand in front of Annie's face. "I just did the best impression of Robins half-cut on cheap wine, and you missed it because you were too busy staring right at the wall."

Swift started pacing up and down beside the table, wobbling to and fro and pulling his lips into a tight smile.

"I like Robins," Annie said with a wry smile. "She's a grown-up, intimidating version of Malibu Barbie."

Swift grimaced, dropping into a seat where he stood.

"Yeah," he nodded. "I like her too. So? What were you dreaming about? Or do I not want to know?"

Annie felt a blush rise in her cheeks. Swift was a friend now, a good friend, but he didn't need to know that people were gossiping about who she'd slept with to get her job.

"I was just thinking about Mim." Annie downed her wine and leant over the table for the bottle to top her glass up.

"How is your sister?" Swift pushed his cup towards Annie and the gentle glug of the wine filled the silence Annie was leaving.

After almost twenty years not knowing where her baby sister had ended up, Mim had thrown herself back into Annie's life, and brought with her a whole new perspective on what happened to them as children.

"Oh, you know," Annie replied, chewing her cheek. "Still trying to get me to remember how brilliant my dad was and how my mum is a ruthless killer. Same old. Same old."

Annie looked up from her Malbec and right into the blue eyes of her boss. Swift's brows were knotted, his lips pursed.

"I can't tell if you're joking or not," he said, pulling his chair down the table towards her, he leant in, scrutinising her face.

Annie could smell his aftershave, spicy and rich, and it was comforting. He'd been her rock these last couple of years and she felt her stomach shrink a little at the proximity.

"Me neither, to be honest." She forced out the words with a croak. "It's *apparently* all true, but also bat-shite crazy. So, there we go."

Swift dropped back in his chair, blowing air out pursed lips. "Woah. I know you said Mim coming back had brought with it some difficulties, but that's… I dunno, insane. No wonder you're not up for a party. Do you want to talk about it?"

Annie's shoulder slumped with the relief of having told Swift the truth. Having Mim back in her life was amazing, but intense.

"Nah." She shook her head. "Sorry, I shouldn't have dragged you away from the hubbub just because I can't be doing with it right now."

"Are you kidding?" Swift pulled the platter of food towards them and popped a prawn in his mouth. "I have food, wine, and reasonable company. There's nowhere I'd rather be right now."

Annie pushed gently at Swift's shoulder. "Oy, I'm great company." She looked around the incident room, with its off-white walls, empty fabric notice-board, and a whiteboard that still held remnants of its past cases smudged into indecipherable rainbows. "And if there's nowhere you'd rather be, right now, I'd say you need to get out more."

She gave him a cheeky smile and helped herself to some more wine as the door swung open and Tink and Page toppled in.

"I told you they'd run off." Page's youthful face had the flush of alcohol as he ducked his tall frame into the room. It was the first time Annie had seen him wearing a shirt and tie and it suited him, even though his muscles were trying to break free.

Tink had on a sparkly number which she'd complimented with an equally dazzling headband across her bleached pixie cut. She grabbed Page's tie and dragged him in the room, shutting the door firmly behind her.

"Robins is looking for you," she whispered, as sober as the rest of them, which was not very. "*Us*. She's looking for all of us."

She giggled and grabbed the bottle of wine, swigging straight from the open neck.

"Is that why you're hiding?" Page asked, taking

the bottle from Tink and having a swig himself.

"No," Tink giggled. "Look at them all cosy. I'm sure Robins has nothing to do with them running off together."

Annie felt her face flush and she pushed her chair a little away from Swift's as she noticed his cheeks redden too. Tink leant into Page, holding her hand up to hide her words the way primary school children do.

"I told you," she said, in an almost whisper, winking at Page as she spoke.

At least, Annie thought it was a wink, it was hard to tell past the drunkenness.

"I think you've had enough of that." Swift took the bottle from Page as he broke down in giggles. "How about going to get us all a cup of coffee?"

Page drew his bottom lip into his mouth, reprimanded and trying not to laugh.

"If Robins wants to find us all I'm guessing it's not to ask us to join her in a game of Twister," Swift added, grimly.

"You'd be right about that."

The four members of the MCU turned to look at the door. Robins stood there, hands on hips, her own tailored suit had a dusting of sparkle running through it, making her a glitter ball who was giving off menacing vibes along with her Chanel.

"Robins, hi," Swift said, eyeing up their boss, slowly moving the bottle of wine behind his back. "Having a good evening?"

DCI Robins stepped into the room and closed the

door behind her. Annie stood up, the room felt small with five bodies in it, and she didn't want to be at a disadvantage as the only one still sitting down.

"I was," Robins said. "But I've just received a call that put a dampener on it. I need you all to sober up, I've got a job for you."

"But it's a Friday night, and we're at a party," Swift moaned. "Can't you get the night team on it?"

"Whose party are you at?" Robins puffed her chest. "Because as far as I can see, this is an MCU party and no-one else is invited. Have you even said hello to Malcolm?"

She looked at Annie for this one. Annie glanced at Swift, mouthing the name at him.

"Malcolm," Robins said again, louder. "You know, the guy whose party this is? Served with the force for thirty years."

"Oh, yeah, Malcolm," Annie smiled. "Of course we have."

She had no idea what Malcolm looked like.

"What's up?" Swift was in work mode; Annie could tell by the way he was looking at Robins, the hunger in his eyes for a new case.

Robins strode around the table and stood at the front of the room.

"You'd better sit down," she gestured in front of her. "Especially DC Page, you look like you might hit the deck at any moment."

The flush on Page's face had turned very slightly green and he grimaced at the platter of food as he sat at the table. Tink helped herself, clearly still in the happy stages of her evening.

"Okay," Robins started. "We've had notification of a young woman walking around Everly Park causing damage to the bandstand."

"What kind of damage?" Annie asked, curious as to why MCU were being tasked with a possible criminal damage charge. That was normally left to the beat officers.

"Graffiti," Robins replied.

"So why come to us?" Swift asked, obviously feeling the same way as Annie. "Is it a hate crime too?"

Robins shook her head. "She's written a verse from Shakespeare; *Vengeance is in my heart, death in my hand.*"

"Titus Andronicus," Tink said, flaky pastry resting on the top of her lips. "Not one of his best, but I think it's a bit late to involve MCU for his literary crimes now."

Robins' lips tightened and Tink sank lower on her chair.

"The damage and the quote aren't the reason I want you involved," she said, wearily. "The woman in question looks disturbed and scared. But you would be too if you had a bomb strapped around your chest."

The room quietened; Annie could have heard a pin drop until Page opened his mouth to speak the words they were all thinking.

"Holy crap," he muttered.

TWO

THE RETIREMENT PARTY HAD DONE THE MCU A favour. None of the team looked like police officers, rather they blended in with the regular city goers of a Friday evening. Annie drew her coat around her shoulders as she stepped down from Swift's car. She'd swapped her usual waterproof mac dotted with holes for a faux fur number mimicking a snow leopard, and with her pleather leggings and heeled boots, Annie felt like heading to the pub and continuing the drinking. Especially as Swift was looking pretty dapper himself.

"Right, you guys, over here." Robins drew Annie back to the cold night and the alleyway they'd parked in out of sight.

Annie, Swift, Tink, and Page gathered round the cruisers that had their lights and sirens off. The alleyway was quiet, the chatter of police radios cut occasionally splitting the air. Annie's breath clouded and she could smell the faint tinge of cigarettes as she neared Robins.

"We don't know who this woman is yet," Robins said, popping a polo mint between her lips. "We don't know if she's a member of a terrorist cell or working alone. There have been no other sightings of possible partners in the city this evening, but the whole force is on high alert for the possibility of a planned, simultaneous attack."

Annie shivered. The cold was bad enough, but Robins' words cut deeper.

"What's the plan?" asked Swift.

"We've stepped up uniformed patrols," Robins continued. "And alerted the bomb disposal unit, the EOD squad. As you all are aware, unless you're the Met, no police force in the UK has the resources for its own bomb squad, so we're awaiting ETA on that. In the meantime, I want to use your excellent disguises to our advantage."

"Guv?" Tink asked, her dress glittering under a streetlight.

"You all look like you're heading for a night on the tiles," Robins clarified. "So, I want you to head off in pairs to the park and act like normal citizens. Get the low-down and report back here. Do not get close to the perp and do not approach. Like I said, act normal."

"Easier for some than others," Tink muttered cheekily, and Annie thought she must still be drunk.

"DS Lock, do I need to dunk you in a bath of cold

19

water to sober you up?" The tip of Robins' nose was turning pink. "Because I am happy to do it."

Tink shook her head. "No, sorry Guv, I'm on it. Sober as a… sober thing."

Robins rolled her eyes. "It's a good job most of the other teenagers out there are as pissed as you are."

"I'm almost twenty-seven I'll have you know," Tink pulled her shoulders back and eeked out her full five foot three inches.

"Page, take Tink and head off across the north side of the park." Robins ignored Tink. "And Swift, you and Annie pretend to be a couple and head down the south side. The bandstand is in the middle so you should all get a good view of the perp. And remember. Do. Not. Approach."

Swift offered up his elbow and Annie linked her arm through his, feeling the heat from his body through her coat sleeve. They watched Tink and Page stumble off towards the road, waiting a couple of minutes to give them a head start, then took off out of the alleyway.

"What are your first thoughts?" Annie asked, trying to hold still her shivers, never having come across anything terror related before.

Swift cleared his throat and steered them across the empty road and onto the walkway to Everly Park. There were a few groups of people milling around the roads, though they were on the fringes of the bustling city centre where most of the revellers would be found. Streetlights dotted the pavement with pools of orange, and Annie and Swift continued down through the paths that circled the edges of the park.

"Honestly," Swift replied as they started walking slowly down around the bottom of the park. "I have no idea. If this woman is wearing a bomb, why is she vandalising the place when she's just going to blow it up?"

"Not helping with my *about to be blown up* anxiety there Swift," Annie said, gripping his elbow tightly with her arm. "But you're right. I don't get it either. If she's tagging the place before she... does it, then maybe she's not going to detonate it right here, maybe first she's alerting the authorities who's responsible."

"By quoting Shakespeare?" Swift led them off the main path and onto a smaller paved area that cut through the centre of the park.

In the distance Annie could see the bandstand; a couple of groups of young people mingled around, swigging from cans and oblivious to the danger that may be encroaching upon them. The air clouded around their faces, their breath hot against the night, their body temperature ramped up by alcohol and hormones. Annie dug her free hand into her pocket to keep it warm.

"Are there any terror cells who have an affinity to the bard?" she asked, watching a lone woman around her own age walk away from the bandstand, her arms wrapped tightly around her body.

Annie tensed, there was something about the

woman that set her apart from the crowd. The way she was walking, tense and upright, her head sweeping back and forth across the wide expanse of grass, eyes so wide that even in the darkness they caught the lamplight.

"Keep walking," Swift whispered, tugging gently at Annie's arm. "Don't draw attention to her or us. We'll sweep back around and see where she goes, but only once she's passed us by."

Annie's legs felt like jelly and she was glad of the crutch of Swift's arm to hold on to. She didn't know where to look as the woman approached them. Would she normally smile and say hello at a stranger in a park? Not at night time, but Annie needed to look, to see what was written on the face of the woman who could probably end the lives of her and Swift and a bunch of teenagers with the flick of a switch.

She held her breath as the woman passed by, her lungs aching by the time she was out of eyesight.

"Definitely her," Annie said, quietly, forcing herself not to look back. "Come on, quick, we need to get back around to see where she goes."

Annie pulled at Swift's arm, forcing him to speed up. They marched all the way around the bandstand, ignoring the loud chatter from the teenagers, and back onto the path. There was no sign of Tink or Page, and the police vehicles were out of sight so as not to raise suspicions, but Annie watched as plain clothes officers made their way smoothly around the park, gathering up anyone who could be in danger and moving them quietly out beyond the gates.

"Did you get a good look at her?" Swift asked as they rounded the path to the lower part of the park. "Can you tell by looking at her how likely she is to press the switch?"

There was a wobble to Swift's question and Annie opened her mouth to try to say something reassuring when his phone vibrated in his pocket. They slowed down so Swift could lift it out and check and all the while Annie was trying not to think about how little time they may have and whether answering a phone was the best way to spend it.

"It's Robins," Swift said, swiping his screen and illuminating his face in an eerie blue glow "Shit."

Annie's shoulders twitched. "What is it?"

"We've got the ETA for the EOD and they're over forty-eight hours away." Swift tapped out a reply and pocketed his phone.

"Forty-eight hours?" Annie winced. "Let's hope she's not used Wilco batteries for the timer because that baby will be going off before the EOD get up the A11."

It was a bad time to be making jokes but after almost two years in the team, Annie was using gallows humour on a daily basis.

"So… what happens now?" Annie continued as they started off again.

Swift cleared his throat and held his arm out for Annie's.

"They're sending in armed units," he said as Annie once again made her arm comfortable in the crook of his elbow.

"Armed units?" she almost shouted. "So just because the bomb squad can't make it, what, we shoot her?"

They stepped out from a small copse of bushes and there she was. Sitting on a bench staring unblinkingly out across the grass. Annie followed her view but saw nothing but an expanse of darkness.

"Swift," Annie whispered. "We need to do something."

"Let's walk past her again, see if we can see a way to overpower her," he whispered back. "We can report back to patrol, see if they can help. Anything is better than resorting to a power struggle between a bomb and a gun."

Annie felt a shudder through his sleeve and had to force herself to draw breath. Their footsteps were silent in the night, drawn away as though by the darkness itself. Annie tried to stomp a little, just to give the woman warning that they were approaching her. The last thing they need now was to startle someone so unstable and creeping up on her when she looked in such a dreamlike state would be likely to do just that. It didn't work, though the trance the woman was in gave Annie the opportunity to study her face.

Steely eyed, the woman kept her gaze right out in front of her. Her face was grey, not even warmed by the orange from the park lights. Dark circles highlighted her wide eyes. Her mouth was drawn in on itself, the tiny sliver of lip that was still visible was blue. There was something in her hands that she was gripping so tightly it turned her knuckles white and the backs of her hands mottled. Round and round her fingers twisted as though mesmerised by whatever it was she held.

The charge?

But there was something else written on the woman's face, something Annie couldn't quite grasp. Was it resoluteness? Maybe it was acceptance.

They walked closer, the bench only a few feet away. Annie felt her head swim with the shallow breaths she'd been taking, just as the woman turned her head and caught her eye. And before Annie could look away the woman gave her a very slight shake of her head and Annie realised what it was she'd seen, anger.

"What are you doing?" Swift hissed at Annie as she drew her arm out of his. "O'Malley, you've been given strict instructions to *observe* only. If you approach, I'll bloody kill you myself."

Annie hoped she knew what she was doing and figured if she didn't then it wouldn't be Swift killing her. She also hoped it would be quick.

"Oh my god, hi." Annie turned her attention to the woman and threw her arms up in a big wave. "How are you? I haven't seen you in ages I almost didn't recognise you."

Please work, please work.

"You're in deep shit, O'Malley." Swift backed away to the edge of the path, never letting Annie out of his sight.

The bench was cold under her trousers as Annie sat down. She could feel the dampness seep into her skin but that was nothing compared with the iciness she felt running through her brain that she'd misread the situation. Maybe the anger she'd seen flash across the woman's face was anger at the world she was about to blow up and not anger at what had happened for her to end up in a park strapped up with explosives.

There was only one way to find out.

THREE

"WHAT ARE YOU DOING?" THE WOMAN SPAT AT Annie, drawing her coat tightly around her chest.

Annie could barely hear the woman's hissing voice over the sound of her own thumping heart. She ignored the warning glares and the stomping of Swift's feet as he took off to a safe distance to observe.

"How are you?" Annie over emphasised her words and movements so to a stranger watching, they'd look like old friends. "It's been an age."

Annie raised her brows at the woman, coaxing her to talk. Up close the fear was more pronounced, written on her face with the pallor of her skin and her pinprick pupils. But the anger still flared, and Annie could tell she was about to become a victim to it as the woman drew her face into a twisted smile. Annie's insides flipped over themselves, and she felt the acidic alcohol bubble up her gullet.

"What are you doing?" The woman hissed again, trying to force the smile to stay. "I don't know who the hell you are, but if you don't get the hell away from me then neither of us will be around long enough to find out."

Annie flinched as she leant in towards her.

"What do you mean?" she asked.

"There's a bomb strapped to my body." The woman's eyes bored into Annie's.

Annie sat up straighter, trying not to shiver at the coldness now numbing her fingers and toes.

"We know," she hissed back, her smile slipping slightly. "Why do you think I'm here? The police know, the whole park is surrounded. Every person you see walking around the park right now is a police officer. There's no way out for you. I maybe shouldn't be telling you this before I've confirmed to myself that I'm safe, but the bomb squad is miles away so they're bringing in the armed unit instead. Whichever way you look at it, that's *not* good for you."

The woman's bottom lip wobbled, and she drew it painfully far into her mouth tracing red marks across her skin.

"You can't let them shoot me." Her eyes searched Annie's face frantically. "It's not my bomb. I don't want to hurt anyone. Please, you have to help me."

Annie grabbed the woman's shaking hands and held them in her own. She couldn't tell who was the coldest.

"Look at me," she said, kindly. "Just smile and

28

pretend like we're long-lost friends. I'm trying to work out how to get you out of here alive. Trust me, please."

"Okay." The woman drew a stuttered breath. "Thank you."

"Let's start with your name," Annie asked. "So I know what to call you."

"Jessica," she replied. "Jessica Frampton."

Jessica reeled off her date of birth and her home address, her shoulders tensed around her neck.

"My sister should be home," Jessica said. "We're supposed to be going out tonight. We've not been out in so long. She's going to be worried about me."

"Thank you, Jessica," Annie said, shaking Jessica's hands in hers like two friends who were sharing an exciting secret. "I'm Annie."

"Are you police?" Jessica asked.

Annie nodded. "I'm a psychotherapist, but I work for the police force." She looked over at Swift who was pink around the gills. "Perhaps not for much longer though, given the state of my boss over there. We were under strict instructions not to approach you. Whoops."

Jessica gave a puff of a laugh. "Why did you? Approach me, I mean? If you knew I was a ticking time bomb?"

Annie lowered their hands and slid her own back into her pockets. "Something about this whole situation didn't sit right with me. Why were you graffitiing a park you're about to blow up? Where's the point in

29

that? Then when Swift and I were walking past you, the look on your face gave you away, I guess."

"I can see why the police hired you," Jessica said, the side of her lips lifting in a real smile.

"Let's wait until I can work out a way to get you home safe before you say that," Annie replied, running her eyes over Jessica for wires or any clues to pass on to Robins about what type of explosive they were dealing with.

It was no good, the young woman's coat covered her from chin to knees, any bulkiness was hidden by the material.

"We've probably only got a couple of minutes before whoever did this starts to get suspicious." Jessica glanced around the park. "I don't know how but I think he's watching me."

Annie nodded. "That's why I did what I did, I had to pretend to know you, or I'd blow our cover."

"Or me *up*." Jessica laughed at Annie's poor turn of phrase.

"Sorry," Annie said, grimacing. "What can you tell me about the device?"

Jessica chewed on the inside of her cheeks, her eyes wide.

"It's heavy, really heavy," she said. "It's like a life jacket, which is ironic, but with packs of stuff stuck to the sides of it. I don't know what it is, or what it's packed with, and there are no off switches, trust me, that was the first thing I looked for when I woke up."

"Can you tell me what happened?" Annie asked,

mentally taking notes. "How did you end up strapped with explosives?"

"Someone jumped me on my way home from work," Jessica replied. "I have no idea who or why. I woke up in my car and I was rigged up. I wasn't even out for that long, a couple of hours at most, but the bastard took my phone and my bag, so I had no way of getting in touch with anyone. When I woke up it was still dark, and I felt like I'd been hit over the head with a sledge hammer. I guess that must have been from whatever he knocked me out with."

"You keep saying *he,*" Annie questioned. "Could you tell it was a he?"

Jessica shook her head. "I have no idea, but I can't imagine a woman doing this, can you?"

Annie thought back to some of the other cases she'd worked on with Swift and could very much picture a woman doing this, but she kept her mouth shut.

"Any other family we need to inform?" she asked instead.

Jessica's eyes filled with tears, and she wiped them away hurriedly with the back of her hand.

"I have to get back for my son," she whispered, her voice catching in her throat. "He's all I've got."

Annie's stomach clenched. "Where is he now? Is he safe?"

Jessica nodded briskly. "He's with his dad, we're not together anymore." She gave a quick shake of her head to Annie's raised eyebrow. "No way. For a start he's not got it in him to hurt me. We're okay, you know, as exes. Plus, this is way too complex for him. Why wait a year just to strap me to some explosives when he could have popped me some pills and dunked me in a bath, you know?"

Annie grimaced, "true."

"Plus," Jessica added, with an ironic smile. "He'd have to care for our baby all by himself and he's way too selfish to want to do that. Pretty sure he enjoys being a part-time dad, you know?"

"Okay," Annie agreed, noticing Swift as he paced a few feet away, his hands gripped tightly in his pockets. "So, any other ideas? Anyone else out there who'd wish to harm you? Anyone extreme enough to go to these lengths?"

Jessica laughed, a proper belly laugh that took Annie by surprise.

"Oh god," Jessica said, wiping a tear away from the corner of her eye with purple fingers. "How long have you got?"

"I think that's more a question that should be directed at you," Annie looked pointedly at Jessica's bulky waistline.

"Yes, of course, sorry," Jessica sighed. "Look, I'm a barrister. I work as a prosecutor for the Crown. If you want to know who has a vendetta against me, you'll need to look up a list of people I've successfully put away. And it's long."

Annie watched as Jessica folded in on herself. Her shoulders slumped forwards as though she, too, was just figuring out this was going to be a needle in a haystack case. Annie tried to look as bright as she could, but alongside the growing unease at the list of suspects, there was something else niggling at her. Something that didn't add up. She wracked her brains, but the cold had seeped into her cranium and was freezing her little grey cells.

The sound of Swift's footsteps drew Annie's eyes away from Jessica's face and towards her boss. He looked as cold as Annie felt.

"Hello, *dear*," he said, stuttering with what Annie hoped was just the cold and not deep repressed anger at her. "We need to be making a move, soon, our... um... friends have arrived. Finally."

He dropped his voice and added, "apparently they got lost on the way to the park even though they'd been given comprehensive directions."

That was it.

Annie span back around to Jessica, aware of what had been irritating her, ignoring Swift's annoyed muttering.

"You said the perp took your bag and phone," Annie said, and Jessica nodded. "So, why were you vandalising the bandstand? Why did you come here?"

"To the park?" Jessica asked.

"Yes."

"I was told to come here."

"How?" Annie's stomach churned with anxiety.

"There was a phone in my coat pocket." Jessica

went to take it out, but Annie shook her head almost imperceptibly.

"Not here, not where we might be being watched. But can you try to find the number of the phone he's given you so we can track down where he might have purchased it from?"

"It started to ring when I woke up," Jessica said, nodding. "When I answered there was a voice. It sounded a bit like Ghost Face, you know, from Scream. All distorted and weird."

"Go on." Swift had moved closer, he perched on the bench beside Annie, a warm arm around her shoulders.

She almost leant into him before remembering that it was just for show, they were pretending to be a couple so whoever was watching them didn't get suspicious.

"He told me I'd find the cans under my car seat." Jessica's voice wobbled. "That I needed to come straight here and spray paint the walls of the band-stand with the words *Vengeance is in my heart. Death in my hands.* That he had a night of chaos planned for me and I had to do everything he told me to or…"

Tears threatened at the edges of Jessica's green eyes, and she sucked in air through pursed lips.

"Or?" Swift prompted.

"Or he'd flip the switch and blow me up. And then he'd go after my family."

Annie's stomach dropped; a rollercoaster pitching over the crest and plummeting towards the ground.

34

"Look," Annie said, trying to swallow away her fear. "I know this is weird, but can we pretend we're taking a selfie? I'd like you to open your coat a little, just so we can get a glimpse of the vest. The more we know about it, the better chance we have of..."

Annie stopped. She was going to say *of getting you out alive* but was it fair to remind Jessica that the opposite was more plausible? Jessica shuffled into Annie and let her arms drop, her coat flapped open only slightly, but enough for Annie to catch a glimpse of a bunch of colourful wires wrapped in duct tape. She smiled for the phone camera and snapped off a few photos.

"I'm so scared." Jessica's hands were shaking. "Do you think I'll be okay?"

And in the silence left by Jessica's words, the sound of a phone ringing echoed out from her coat pocket.

The three looked at each other, wide eyed. Swift grabbed Annie's arm and dragged her off the bench, throwing his arm around her shoulder and gripping her tightly.

"Do as he tells you," Swift said, looking back at Jessica. "But you're not on your own anymore."

As Annie was marched away from the young woman strapped with explosives, she heard the phone's ring tone cut out and a scared voice speak.

"What's next?"

FOUR

IF ANNIE THOUGHT SWIFT HAD LOOKED ANGRY AT her, that was nothing compared to Robins. Their normally composed DCI had turned a shade of purple, only enhanced by the orange glow of the streetlights overhead. But it was the single strand of hair sticking up at an awkward angle that really gave the game away. Annie took a deep breath and stepped up to meet her fate.

"What did you think you were doing?" Robins hissed; her lips pursed. "You'd better have a bloody good explanation as to why you deliberately went against protocol, putting not only the whole job in jeopardy but also your life. And Swift's."

Annie glanced at Joe who was busy inspecting the skin around his thumb. She hadn't considered for a moment that she'd put his life in danger and an apology almost crossed her lips. But Annie held it in, she didn't want to give any credence to Robins' anger by admitting what she had done was wrong. Mostly because she didn't think it was.

"You hired me because of my people reading skill, yes?" she said, instead, silently dying a little inside at her forwardness.

"Don't make me regret that." Robins' nostrils flared but she was returning to her normal shade of pale.

"Something about the whole situation didn't sit right with me, not when I saw the woman's face." Annie cocked her head to Swift and looked around for Tink and Page.

"They're not back yet," Robins interjected, seeing Annie's questioning look.

With Swift by her side, Annie nodded and continued, her breath pluming in front of her face.

"Her name is Jessica Frampton, she's twenty-eight years old and she has a young son who is staying with his father at the moment." Annie reeled off Jessica's address and Robins dipped her head. "Jessica is a prosecutor for the Crown and was attacked in the car park of the courts earlier this evening. She is fitted with an unknown explosive device that is linked to the perp. A vest, she said, heavy, with wires, but that was all she knew. I've got a photo; I'll send it to the tech team. The perp has given her a mobile phone and is instructing her to do tasks through that. She's going to find out the number and let us know somehow. If she fails to follow his instructions then Jessica, and all those near her will be blown up. He also told her he'd go after her family."

Robins' eyes were wide as Annie finished talking. She plucked her phone from her pocket and swiped the screen with leather gloves, giving Jessica's address and instructions to search her property to whoever was on the other end.

"We need to pull back on the bomb squad," Annie went on. "Whoever it is giving Jessica the instructions is watching her, if we go in all guns blazing then she's going to die."

Robins drew her lips into her mouth, risking the immaculate lipstick she always wore.

"Good work, O'Malley, Swift," she said, giving them a single nod. "Go set up an incident room back at the station. We need to gather information about all Ms Frampton's recent cases, her family, this ex-partner. I'll send Tink and Page there too when they return."

The tight band that had been twisted around Annie's chest since she sat down with Jessica had finally loosened and with it the adrenaline was dissipating. Annie felt an onslaught of coldness hit her and she shivered violently. Swift wrapped his arm around her shoulders, softly this time, warming her, not dragging her away. He whispered something in her ear but with the racing blood thumping and the mass of her curls in the way, she didn't quite catch what he said.

"Go get in the car and warm up," Robins continued. "We'll need to get eyes on Jessica, and we'll need to do it carefully, no uniforms. But we need to know where she's going next, be one step ahead of the perp. I'll get a uniform on it, make out they're a beat officer and they need to keep their distance. Dammit."

"There's no need," Annie said, her teeth chattering. "I slipped my AirTag into Jessica's pocket while we were sat on the bench. I can keep an eye on her movements through my phone."

Robins' eyebrows shot skywards. "Brilliant, well done, O'Malley. I'll give your details to the tech team, and they can trace her too. Now go and get a coffee. We need you sharp as a tack and just as painful."

Robins spun on her heels and headed towards where the ARU vans had pulled into the side street. Swift blew out a stream of air and squeezed Annie's shoulders.

"You gave me a fright back there, O'Malley." He led her to his car and unlocked the doors. "But that was good work. I'm impressed."

"Thanks," Annie replied, climbing into the passenger side, and waiting not so patiently for Swift to turn on the heated seats. Frost had started to form on the windshield, patterning the glass in a cobweb of sparkles. "There's no need to sound so surprised, though."

She tried to give Swift a cheeky smile, but her face was so cold the muscles weren't playing ball.

"Not surprised," Swift said, closing his door and turning over the engine. Warm air started to blast through the vents and Annie felt the seat under her warming. "Just relieved."

He reversed out of the side street and they made their way back to the station in a comfortable silence, Annie's brain working like a cryptic lock trying to unpick all of the clues that Jessica had told her during their short spell in the park. She'd been attacked near the courts, her place of work where she spent hours tirelessly prosecuting people who mostly ended up in prison. The perp had masked his identity—and Jessica had been sure it had been a man—though Annie knew they had to keep an open mind. Jessica was a pawn in a sick game of dare, and whoever was pulling the strings wanted to do it anonymously, so at the moment there were no links to any terrorist cells or local extremist groups.

Graffiti wasn't the worst crime in the world and spraying the works of Shakespeare onto a bandstand seemed a little middle class to Annie. They pulled into the car park of the station and Annie was none the wiser, nothing about the evening was making sense yet, but it was early days.

A skeleton staff kept the station alive after hours. Annie's best friend, Rose, was manning the desk as O'Malley and Swift walked in out of the cold. Rose looked up from her magazine and tilted her chin at the officers.

"You're up late," she said, licking her forefinger and turning the page.

"New case," Annie replied, glad of the blast of

warm air from the heaters above the door. "We'll be here all night I should think."

"Cosy." Rose winked and Annie felt her cheeks heat as she skipped to catch up with Swift as he swiped his pass card and left the reception. "Let's do coffee soon, O'Malley, it's been an age."

Annie raised an arm in acknowledgement and squeezed past Swift as he held open the door for her.

"What about my invite," he shouted back to the receptionist who blew him a kiss and went back to reading.

The corridor was empty, the open plan office dead too. They stopped at the doors, an eerie glow from one of the computers at the far end reflected off the dark windows and illuminated everything in an off-white cloak. Despite the lack of people, the smell of the party was still strong. The tang of champagne and a hint of red wine, the sweaty smell of finger food left in the open.

"O'Malley," Swift said, letting the door to the open plan office shut, keeping him and O'Malley out in the corridor. "Why don't you go and find us an empty incident room and I'll whip us up something hot to drink."

Annie gave Swift a salute and carried on down the corridor.

There were four incident rooms, gradually decreasing in size the further into the building they went. Peeking through the door to rooms one and two, Annie saw the makings of complex cases littering the noticeboards and covering the tables. She rounded the corner into the darkness, waving her arms around at the ineffective lighting sensors until they flooded the space with a gloomy glow.

Pushing the door to the third room open, Annie flicked the switch on and smiled at the blank blue pin board and the empty tables. She threw her bag on the nearest chair and slid her feet out of her heeled boots, sighing at the comfort of the carpet under her bruised heels. At five foot eight, Annie didn't often wear heels, and she hadn't expected to be wearing her party shoes for a stroll around the park. She twisted the blinds shut and propped open the door with a chair so Swift would know where to find her.

There was a marker on the shelf under the white-board; Annie pulled off the lid and tested a small dot in the corner of the screen to make sure it was wipeable before setting to work. Writing Jessica's name in the middle of the board, Annie added around it, filling up the white space with a spidery chart list full of questions with no answers.

"Tink and Page are back in the building," Swift said, making Annie jump. "Tink looks a little worse for wear. Sorry, I didn't mean to scare you, you looked in your own world there."

With pen covering the tips of her fingers, Annie grabbed a cup of milky coffee with thanks and stood back next to Swift to look over her work.

"Poor Tink," she said, remembering how many pre-party drinks the young DS had consumed to give her the energy to make the party in the first place. Confiding in Annie, Tink had mentioned at least a couple Margaritas and a Sex on the Beach. "Hopefully the fresh air helped."

"No, no it definitely didn't help." Tink came into the room with less enthusiasm than normal, bringing with her the subtle aroma of alcohol mixed with the less subtle acidity of vomit. "Poor Page had to hold my hair out my face."

The tall DC stood behind her with a raised eyebrow. "You're lucky you have no hair, Tink. Because I wouldn't have been anywhere near your face when you were offloading in the hedge."

They both had the rosy cheeks of children coming in from playing in the snow. Tink threw herself onto a chair and dropped her head into her arms on the table. Page gave her a friendly pat on the shoulders and walked to the other end of the table before he took his own chair.

"I'm not great with sick." He waved his hands in Tink's general direction as reasoning enough for his distance.

"Tink," Swift said, grimacing. "Can you stick to the soft drinks in future?"

"I didn't know we were going to be on a case, did I?" she said, her voice muffled into her arms. "I thought we were toasting the farewells of Marty, and I wanted to make sure I gave him a good send off. It wouldn't be fair on him if I'd have stuck to the lemonade now, would it? Much better to toast him with a glass of fizz."

Swift chuckled and walked to the front of the room. Annie pulled out the chair near Tink and quickly changed her mind, moving to near Page instead. He smelt like candy floss and cold winters.

"Malcolm," Swift said, picking up the pen Annie had been using.

"What?" she asked, wondering if somewhere between entering the building and making the coffees Swift had solved the case.

"It was *Malcolm's* retirement do, we don't have a Marty working in Norfolk Constabulary."

Tink muttered something that sounded like *whatever* from under her arms, and Annie saw Swift's mouth lift in a grin.

"As punishment for your lushness," Swift went on. "I need you to make a list of all of Jessica's recent cases, get the details of her ex, any family, do a thorough sift. And do it ASAP; we don't know if this explosive is also on a timer."

"Guv," Tink replied, lifting her head, the smile she gave Swift would not have melted an iceberg.

"Page," he went on. "We need you to…"

The sharp trill of Annie's mobile cut through Swift's words.

"O'Malley," she said, answering Robins, all eyes on her.

"She's on the move," Robins replied. "Get your

team mobile. Follow the tag and find out what she's doing next."

"On it." Annie hung up and looked to Swift.

"We need eyes on Jessica at all times. Someone who hasn't been seen with her already this eve." Swift swung his head between Tink and Page. "Someone who doesn't smell like a bar fight at 6am. Page, it's your time to shine."

FIVE

AMERICAN PIE

IT HAD BEEN A GOOD FIVE YEARS SINCE DC TOM Page had frequented a Tesco Metro in the early hours of a Saturday morning, but the clientele hadn't changed. Pretending to peruse the magazine aisle, Page could spot the clubbers, warmed enough by alcohol to not need coats, giggling sporadically near the heated pies and pasties. There were the shift workers grabbing coffee, crisps, and dips. And the less fortunate counting out their coins for a bottle of cheap cider to see them through the next day.

Page picked up a copy of yesterday's local paper and pretended to read the sports page and the gloomy headlines of relegation battles. He knew he could very well have been in a different position, counting out his own pennies instead of on a police stakeout. As a young boy, Page had been classic bully material, short, stout, with a crew cut and baggy clothes. No one knew that he was short and stout because his parents fed him on a beige diet of MacDonalds and Chippies, and that was only when they could be bothered to feed him at all. His hair cut short by his dad to avoid the expense of hairdressers and the constant stream of lice. The clippers scratched his scalp and tore at the skin behind his ears. His clothes baggy because they were hand me downs from cousins and uncles and all the other unidentified males who frequented his home.

Page had taken the mantle of bully because that was what was expected of him, only deep down all he really wanted to do was sit at the front of class and listen to what his teachers were saying. There was a drive to do well, a need to be in school for as long as he could, because the alternative was home, or out on the streets with the unidentified males, peddling whatever it was they had on offer that week.

It was Page's Nan who'd swooped in to help. Super Gran he used to call her, like the TV show they would sit and watch together before settling down to finish his homework. Without the kind heart of his Nan, Page would have carried on the road he was going and ended up on the wrong side of the interview tables he couldn't wait to get to at work.

The doors to the Tesco Metro slid open, bringing with them a blast of cold air and a nudge to Page to concentrate on the work in hand. Glancing over his shoulder he saw who he recognised as Jessica Frampton from the photos Annie had shown him in the car on the way here. She looked blue, her lips cracked and peeling, her arms swaddling her coat tightly around her body. Page went back to his newspaper keeping his wits about him, his senses following Jessica as she walked slowly to the back of the shop. The shelves were too high for Page to see what she was doing, though he hoped that there were no unbalanced drunks too close by.

They'd promised him in the car that the bomb was linked to a perp who was watching from a distance, but there was always a chance that it could detonate by accident. Page knew his job was risky; he weighed up those risks with every case, but those young girls enjoying their night out weren't being given that opportunity and if anything happened to them, Page wouldn't be able to sleep at night.

The pressure of being a normal bystander had been tricky enough in the park, but at least there he'd had the comfort of Tink, no matter how drunk and vomity she'd been. Here he was on his own. Page straightened his shoulders and tucked the paper under his arm. Swift had put him here. Swift trusted him to do his job, and if Swift trusted him then that was more than good enough for Page.

Rounding a shelf stacked with sanitary products and nappies, Page caught sight of Jessica in front of a row of fridges. Her whole body was shaking, through coldness or fear, Page wasn't sure. Looking back by the door, Page saw the security guard had clocked the young woman. They were on alert at this time of night, heightened by the type of customers that walked through the doors, ready to kick people out before the mess hit the fan. Page got out his phone and typed a quick message to Swift.

> Can we get the security guard on board? Target looks like she's attracting attention.

The fridge Jessica was staring at looked as though it had been restocked. Shelves full of Ginsters pasties and pork pies ready for the morning and the early birds picking up a quick lunch. Page sidled past Jessica to the milk and helped himself to a pint.

"It's nippy out, isn't it?" he said, trying his hardest to act like a normal shopper, while also flashing his badge as subtly as possible.

Jessica looked up from the badge into Page's eye and he nearly dropped his milk. He could see the cry for help in the tiny pupils, the redness and he wanted to reach out and draw her close to him.

"Freezing," she said, looking back down at where her hands were wrapped under her armpits.

Lifting her arm for a split second, Page saw what looked like a hypodermic needle gripped tightly in her fingers. Jessica took her free hand and lifted a pasty from the shelf, turning it over in her hands as though she was looking to see what it was made of.

"Well, have a good night," he said, picking up a Ginsters of his own and heading to the self-checkout.

As he scanned his food as slowly as possible, he heard the doors slide open and shut and, turning back, Jessica was nowhere to be seen. Page whipped his phone out of his pocket and dialled Swift.

"We need to seal off this unit," he said, scanning his Ginsters. "I think Jessica may have injected an unknown substance into the baked goods."

"Copy that," Swift replied. "Is the contamination contained?"

"Just the pasties," Page replied, tucking his phone between his ear and his shoulder to pay for his shopping. "Jessica wasn't able to tell me, but she was clear in her actions."

"Can you remain on the scene and keep people away from the substance?" Swift said, and Page could hear him talking to others in the background. "Page, do we think the substance is a biohazard to people standing near it?"

"I don't think so," Page replied, heading back to the fridges, he looked around to check there was no one else in the shop. "Jessica showed me what looked like a syringe, before picking up a brand of pasty. I think she's been tasked to inject something into the goods, not to infect the general public."

"Just to poison one or two." Swift sighed. "Okay, we're on our way. We need to make sure the coast is clear first. The security guard is being brought up to speed as we speak. We'll be thirty minutes tops but we can't afford to be seen."

The call cut off and Page pocketed his phone. New customers were entering the shop and he needed to divert them away from the fridges. He looked around, waiting for inspiration to strike. He didn't want to have to wrestle a delicious snack from the hands of a drunk student, so he needed to keep them away from the fridges completely. They whirred noisily in front of him, condensation dripping down behind the bottles of Irn Bru and Coke and Page wondered for a brief moment if a couple of Mentos and a good shake would cause enough havoc to shut down the fridges. But spotting the plug sockets in between two of the large coolers shut that idea down before it had fully formed. Dropping quickly to his haunches, Page pulled the plug from the wall and watched as the fridge with the sabotaged food fell silent, the light flicking off and throwing the items into darkness.

It was working, but it wasn't quite enough to keep people back. A group of young men dressed in skinny jeans and checked shirts tumbled down the aisle towards him, grabbing each other in an effort to stay upright. Page grabbed a bottle of water and twisted off the lid, tipping the contents on the floor by the fridge.

"I think we've got a problem here," he called back to the security guard. "Can we get some cones out before someone breaks their neck on the water? Watch out lads, mind your step."

One of the young men looked down at the water and back up at Page, hitting his mate on the arm.

"Watch out," he slurred. "He's pissed himself."

The group of men fell about themselves laughing and Page bit his lip and counted to ten. He wasn't about to lose his job because he'd lost his temper. Those day were behind him. It worked, though, even if they did think they were sidestepping a puddle of urine and not pure water from a little stream in North Scotland.

The security guard approached with a glare on his face that had the young men scattering for the crisps. He flipped open a warning sign and placed in on the floor beside the fridge, pulling a grey blind down over the food to stop people taking it.

"Can't have anyone getting dysentery from luke-warm chicken pies now, can we?" he said, in a surprisingly soprano voice. "Now then, why don't you help yourself to a coffee from the Costa machine and I'll keep an eye out here until the... engineer arrives?"

"Right," Page replied, not sure whether to leave the security guard on his own with the evidence or not.

He decided *not* was probably the best way forward and put down his carrier bag and perched on the edge of the fridge. The store had emptied out again, leaving just him, the security guard, and the cashier. Music played softly over the speakers, calming and soporific as Page felt the adrenaline leak from his pores and the tiredness hit. It was the first job he'd been given a trusted front-line role, and Page was quietly proud of himself for the way he'd handled it. As the newbie in the MCU, he knew he had to prove himself, and he was pretty sure he'd done just that. Secured the scene, discovered what had happened, and kept the other shoppers safe, all without alerting the perp to his presence. Page's chest puffed out with pride.

"Careful," the security guard said, nodding at the straining buttons on his dress shirt. "You'll be popping them off if you flex like that again. Flashing your chest at everyone."

"Not while I'm at work, ey?" Page winked at the man and stood to attention as Swift and O'Malley walked through the doors.

SIX

SATURDAY

ANNIE'S ALARM CUT THROUGH HER HEAD LIKE A chainsaw. She hit out at the clock and knocked her glass of water, spilling it all over the floor of her office-cum-flat.

"Crap," she moaned, rolling onto her side in the camp bed and peeling an eye open to see the time. "Double crap."

They'd left the Tesco Metro when the sun had started to rise. With the shop cordoned off and a team of uniforms bagging up the items in the fridge to send off for analysis, Swift had ordered her and Page home to get a few hours' sleep and change into something a little more comfortable. It had only taken Annie five minutes to walk through the city centre to her little flat above the pizza place. Even Pete the pizza man was asleep when she walked past his window, the light off and the shutters drawn.

And now, only three hours later, Annie was dragging herself off the fold up camp bed and up a narrow flight of stairs to her little bathroom in the attic of the old building she called home. After a quick shower, a sweep of her teeth, and a change of clothes she still felt awful but at least she looked slightly better. She grabbed her bag and her phone and headed down the stairs and out into the bright March morning sunshine. The roads were quiet, Annie met the occasional runner and moved out of the way for the sweeping lorry with its circular brushes gathering up the detritus of a Friday night out. Glass bottles clinked against the curb, Styrofoam boxes with half eaten kebabs left a greasy trail as they were sucked into the lorry's belly to be compacted and sent to landfill.

Rose wasn't at the desk as Annie swiped through to the inner sanctum of the station. She waved at the young man who'd replaced her friend for the day shift and headed straight to the incident room they'd set up yesterday. It felt like a week ago, so much had happened since, but it was less than twelve hours. Only the bags under Annie's eyes and the cotton wool feeling in her head could give it away.

"Morning, Annie," Tink greeted her as she pushed open the door to the welcome smell of coffee and pastries. "You're looking as dapper as the rest of the team. Honestly, lightweights, the lot of you."

Tink was sitting crossed legged on the table, her blonde hair brighter than normal, her skin glowing. Swift and Page, in comparison, looked like trolls from under a bridge, folded into their seats cradling Starbucks.

"What gives you the right to look like you've spent the evening in a spa and not puking up the remnants of Marty's retirement do all over the park?" Annie said, dropping her bag on the table next to Tink and grabbing a coffee.

"Matthew," Page corrected, lifting his cup in greeting.

"His name was Malcolm!" Swift rolled his eyes. "And it's no wonder he's leaving if his fellow officers have no idea of his name."

"Can you name every beat officer?" Annie asked, sitting down opposite Swift who raised an eyebrow at her and stood up, the smell of shampoo and citrus filling her nose with the movement. Annie loved that smell; it made her feel safe.

"Okay," he said, running a hand through his hair. "Page, great job last night. The lab is running tox reports on the pasties as we speak, we should hopefully get the results by the end of the weekend, but I'll try to get them fast tracked. Annie, great job to you too, though I was ready to throttle you, you pulled through and because of that we have the vic's name and she wasn't taken out by the ARU. Bonus points for finding out a whistle stop tour of her life too. From that we got her workplace, her family set up, and with that, I think, it's over to you, Tink."

Tink bounced down from the table and grabbed a pile of papers from behind her.

"Okay," she began, Annie still marvelling at how sprightly she looked. "We have Jessica Frampton, twenty-eight, prosecuting barrister for the Crown Courts, cute fringe. Lives with her son in an apartment in the city; a young son, Oliver, who's just turned two, who's with his dad, her ex-partner, Anthony Marble. Has a sister who she was supposed to meet up with last night for a girls' night out.

She's got money, comes with the job. Her car is new. Her apartment is one of the more expensive ones. Her fringe is perfectly trimmed, not a home job, and the upkeep of a neat bob like that isn't cheap. Could it be money motivated?"

"Could be." Annie mulled over the idea that someone would blackmail Jessica by trapping a bomb around her body. "Surely there are easier ways to blackmail someone for money. Her son would be a prime target, for instance. Even though he's at his dad's this weekend. And Jessica ruled out the ex as a possible suspect."

Tink nodded, pinning a picture of Jessica on the noticeboard. "Agreed."

"We need to get eyes on him though," Swift added, furiously scribbling something in his notebook. "Do we have any info on him?"

"Anthony Marble, thirty, still working out what he

does for a living," Tink replied, pinning a social media photo of who Annie assumed was the ex on the noticeboard. He looked like a grown man desperate to still be a teenager. "No priors, but no money either."

"What about her cases?" Page asked, drawing his hand down his chin, and forcing his eyes wider. He looked as tired as Annie felt.

"This is where it gets interesting," Tink went on. She lifted a sheet of paper and started to read a bunch of names. "Harvey Banner, William Baxter, Max Ridle, Alfie Leek. The list goes on. Our girl is good at what she does. There are dozens of names of dangerous criminals who she's successfully prose-cuted and who are now behind bars."

Swift sighed. "That doesn't make our job easy at all. Are there any who have form?"

"I've got a programme searching the database now, any names who match her cases and explosives and we'll know about it in a couple of hours."

"Great work, Tink," Swift said, closing his note-book. "Good comeback from last night."

"Thanks, Guv," Tink replied, giving him a wink, and taking the chair next to Annie.

"Okay." Swift walked over to the noticeboard, Annie's scribbles were still there on the whiteboard beside it, and he paced between the two, perusing the information. "Annie, your questions, do you feel as though any of them have been answered yet?"

Annie looked at what she'd asked herself on the board and shook her head.

"No." She felt at a loss. "We don't know the who, the why, or the how yet. We don't even know if this is linked to Jessica, or if she was just in the wrong place at the wrong time. The suspect may have an ulterior motive that has nothing to do with Jessica. We need to focus on the tasks he's making Jessica do, as well as Jessica herself."

"Agreed," Swift replied. "Tink, look more into the people who Jessica has won against. Check their families, their socials, their bins if you need to. It's more than likely a revenge case, but we need to work out why. Page, put pressure on the lab to get us those tox results, go back to the park and see what else you can glean from the graffiti. Annie, we're going to Jessica's flat to try and work out who she is and why she's ended up the pawn in someone's sick game of dare."

"From what I can tell on my app, Jessica isn't there," Annie said, grabbing a pastry for the car. "Unless she's ditched the tag in a bin in the middle of the city."

"Our officers have been keeping an eye on her," Swift replied. "She's in a coffee shop in the lanes."

"God, poor thing." Tink shook her head, her brows creased. "She must be exhausted. There's only so long adrenaline can keep a person going."

"Which is why it's imperative to get to the bottom of this as quickly as we can," Swift added. "We don't know what's going to be asked of her next, and if she's too exhausted to carry it out then…"

He left the sentence unfinished but the whole team knew what he could have filled in the blanks with. They fell silent, wondering how they could best help her, hoping that their tiredness wouldn't put her life at any more risk than it already was. A seagull landed outside the window, crying loudly, it's throat heaving with the weight of each of its peals. Annie felt like doing the same, there were no easy answers to this case, no way of keeping Jessica safe. There was a young woman out on the streets, petrified, tired, in fear of her life, and scared for everyone around her, and Annie felt helpless. The seagull flapped heavily and took off into the sky with difficulty until it caught on a torrent of air and began to glide. Annie needed her air stream, she needed something to catch a hold of, to pull her along.

"We need to find out more about the bomb," she said, urgently. "We need to know if there's anything we can do to help Jessica before the next dare. Because what if it's something she can't do? What then?"

"What then?" Swift asked, quietly.

The soaring seagull swooped down past the window, cackling loudly, a witch on a broom. Annie gathered together her belongings with a deep sense of foreboding.

SEVEN

JESSICA FRAMPTON'S APARTMENT OVERLOOKED THE river. It was further upstream than the new blocks that had shot up in the early noughties, built in an old, converted factory with proper brick walls and a sturdy feel about it. The door to the block looked to be an original feature, cast from iron and as impenetrable as a castle.

"Do we have a key?" Annie asked Swift as they stood in front of it willing it to open.

"Look at the size of the keyhole," Swift replied, pressing all the buttons on the intercom set into an alcove by the door. "The residents would look like jailers if they needed a key to that thing."

Swift was right, the keyhole was as large as Annie's fist. She ducked down and peered through it but was met with darkness. Of course, it would have been sealed off, these flats cost a fortune and Annie was pretty sure they wouldn't put up with a drafty lobby.

Someone fed up with Swift's incessant pressing of the buttons buzzed them in, Swift pushed at the door and ushered Annie through before the intercom came to life with questions. The inside was disappointingly modern, chip boarded and plain with artwork that looked as though it had come from Ikea. Not offensive, just not what Annie would have pictured from the old brick and iron work outside.

At the far end of the building, beyond the stairwell, set into the wall were a group of post boxes. Annie walked over to it, her shoes echoing on the concrete floor.

"Swift," she said, squinting at the names written on each of the rectangles. "Jessica is apartment four."

"Looks like it's an apartment per floor," he replied, heading for the stairs. "I hope you've had your Weetabix?"

"I've had coffee," Annie said, following him up the stairs. "And no sleep. But that's pretty much the same, isn't it?"

She gave a small laugh and then stopped talking to preserve what little energy she had left. By the time they reached the fourth floor, Annie was ready to lie down and sleep on the concrete, or sign up to a gym membership to rectify her inability to sneeze without feeling like she'd over exerted herself, let alone walk up four flights of stairs. Swift wasn't even breaking a sweat.

"Since when did you get fit?" Annie asked, catching her breath.

Swift shrugged, his cheeks pinkening. "Just thought it was time I started looking after myself. I've been doing the Saturday Park Run."

"Oh." Annie remembered the divorce papers Swift had happily received not that long ago. That's reason enough. She tried not to think about the lead weight sitting on her chest.

"Apartment four," Swift went on, not noticing Annie's discomfort. "Shall we do the old O'Malley and Swift's ten different ways to enter a locked home?"

Thoughts of Swift dating flew from Annie's mind as she studied the apartment door. The small, frosted window set into the thick wood darkened with the unmistakable outline of a person.

"Swift," Annie hissed, pulling him to the side of the door. "There's someone in there."

"Jessica only lives with her son, yes?" he whispered back. "Who's not here at the moment?"

Annie nodded, her heart racing. What if it was the perp? What if he was waiting here for Jessica to come home, or for her to break her promise about contacting the police.

"What do we do?" she asked, listening for signs of life beyond the door.

"We pretend we're coming over for brunch," Swift said, undoing the top button on his shirt and slinging his jacket over his arm. "Come on then, Mrs Swift, let's try to act normal."

Jeez, that's not going to help me act normal. Annie grabbed his arm, and they rounded the door again, Swift knocking as unpolice like as he could.

The window darkened again, the shape moving slowly behind the glass.

"Who is it?" The voice was female, reedy with the tremor of someone scared.

Swift looked at Annie, his eyebrows knotted.

"We're friends of Jessica," Annie replied. "Please can you let us in?"

The clunking turn of the lock was followed by the opening of the door, just an inch, the chain catching before it could go any further.

"She's not here right now," the woman said.

Annie put her at early twenties, she had the same jet-black hair as Jessica only this woman's was long and curled, but it was the eyes that gave her away. As green as freshly steamed broccoli. Annie tried not to laugh as the thought came into her head.

"Are you Jessica's sister?" she asked, moving to give the woman a good view of her face. "Can we come in and have a chat?"

The woman's eyes widened, darting between Swift and Annie.

"Oh god," she said, her hand rushing to the base of her neck. "Oh... has something happened?"

"If you could let us in, we can talk somewhere a

little more private?" Swift said, taking out his badge and showing the woman.

"Jessica is okay, though," Annie added, though not particularly truthfully. She was alive, whether she was okay was probably not up for discussion.

The door slammed shut in their faces. But only moments later, Annie heard the chain moving and this time the door swung open fully. Jessica's sister ushered them inside and checked the landing before closing the door behind them.

"DI Swift, this is Annie O'Malley," Swift said. "Is there somewhere we can sit down?"

"Erinn." The woman nodded and led them through the hallway to a large sitting room with ceiling height windows that looked out over the river. With the polished wooden floors, the subtle but expensive artwork, the Persian rugs, and the minimalist furniture, Annie could get a glimpse of Jessica's real life, and not the petrified, broken woman she'd spent time with the previous night.

"Please take a seat, can I get you a tea or a coffee?" the woman asked, ringing her hands around each other. Her face looked pinched, dark circles surrounded her eyes.

"Coffee would be great, thank you," Annie replied.

Swift nodded and the woman scuttled away.

"What do you think?" Annie asked, when the room was empty. "Definitely has money."

Swift nodded, taking in his surroundings. "That is

an original," he said, motioning towards a giant canvas with shades of cream and white oil paint merged together in a seemingly unpractised hand. "You're looking upward of thirty K."

"I'm sorry, what?" Annie was aghast.

"Yeah," Swift replied. "I've got one in the drawing room at home, Mum bought it years ago."

Whistling through her teeth, Annie started circling the room, looking at the artwork more closely. There were sculptures sitting atop of sideboards, vases on plant stands, the whole room made Annie feel like a child in a proper grown up's house. She stopped at an almost blank canvas, matchbox sized, attached to the wall below a colourful hanging.

"That's taking things a bit too far," she said, bending to look at it more closely. "Is that an original too?"

"An original?" Swift asked, a twinkle in his eye. "That's the intercom system."

Annie felt her face heat and took another look at the canvas. Sure enough, stamped in the very bottom left in the same clean white lines as the rest of the box, was a small intercom icon.

"Oh, well don't I feel stupid?" Annie skulked over to an armchair in a peacock blue and sat with a thump.

Swift laughed, kindly. "You're really cute when you're embarrassed." His face dropped, as though the words had fallen out of his mouth before he'd had a chance to vet them and now he couldn't take them back.

Annie was spared the added embarrassment of having to come up with a reply to that when Erinn returned to the sitting room with a tray of cups. She placed it on a small coffee table made entirely of glass and handed Swift and Annie their drinks.

"Help yourself to milk and sugar," she said, taking one herself and curling into the love seat in front of the large window.

As Annie waited for Swift to take a seat himself, she studied Erinn, the sun behind her making it hard to distinguish her features.

"Sorry to arrive unannounced," Swift began, still standing. "We were under the impression that Jessica just lived with her son."

"Can you tell me what's going on?" Erinn asked, cradling her cup. "Where is Jessica?"

Swift cleared his throat and walked back towards the artwork; Annie saw a shadow cross his face and wondered if he was moving around so he could see Erinn better. He was making her feel slightly unnerved, let alone this young woman whose sister hadn't come home.

"We can't divulge everything right now," he said. "But I can say that your sister is okay."

There it was again, that word. Okay.

"Are *you* okay, Erinn?" Annie asked. "You can talk to us."

Erinn took a sip from her cup, covering even more

of her face. It was disconcerting looking at someone who was all shadows. Annie realised just how much information she gleaned from a person's eyes and mouth, the way they tilted their head or which direction they looked in.

"We were supposed to go out last night, but Jessica never turned up," said Erinn, eventually.

"Did you arrange to meet here? How did you get into her apartment?" Swift was on the move again.

"We normally have a few drinks first." Erinn nodded; Annie could see the movement in her silhouette. "I have a key to this place. I'm in charge of looking after the plants when Jessica goes away."

"Did you try to contact her?" Swift asked.

"Of course I did." Erin's voice wobbled. "I called her so many times, but her phone was going straight to answer machine. You can check my phone if you like."

"That won't be necessary, Erinn, thank you though," Annie intervened.

"Can you think of anyone who might wish Jessica harm?" Swift asked, finally deciding on a dining chair, lifting it, and placing it to the right of Erinn. "Has she spoken of anything weird lately? Anything that's stood out to you about the people she's mentioned? Boyfriends. Girlfriends."

"What's going on?" Erinn was alert now. "Why do you need to know if there are people who would hurt my sister? Where is she?"

"Erinn," Annie spoke up. "We really can't tell you

any more at the moment, but we're doing our best to keep Jessica safe. We really need to know anything you can tell us."

"But there's nothing," Erinn replied. "I don't think she's seeing anyone now. At least, not that she's told me. I did wonder if, when she didn't come home last night, she'd gone back to *his.*"

"His?" Swift prompted.

Erinn scoffed. "Ants. Anthony. Her ex-husband."

"Is that usual for Jessica?" Annie asked.

"God knows," Erinn replied. "But I bloody hope not. He was a useless twat. Out at all hours of the day, Jessica never knew when he'd be home. At least with my other half I know where he is all the time, Ant could have been anywhere," Erinn looked down at her cup. "Sorry for swearing," she added, quietly.

"Swear all you want, Erinn," Swift replied. "We do."

Erinn gave a little laugh and the tension in the air pinged like the popping of a balloon.

"Did you report her missing?" Annie asked, wondering why the alert hadn't made it to their team, the name should have flagged that they were working with the MisPer almost immediately.

"I... oh god, should I have done that?" Erinn asked. "In the end I thought she must be with Oliver, her little boy, because that's the only reason she wouldn't have been in contact. Is he okay? Is it Oliver? Has he been harmed?"

"Oliver is fine as far as we're aware," Annie

replied, making a mental note to check that as soon as they were out of the apartment. "Can you have another think about Jessica, any cases she'd spoken about recently?"

Erinn put down her cup on the parquet flooring and dropped her head into her hands.

"This would be so much easier if you could tell me what the hell's going on." Her voice was muffled.

"Jessica could be in danger," Annie said, trying to make Erinn aware of the urgency of the situation without telling her exactly what was happening. "We need to pinpoint who could wish her harm. And we need to do it quickly."

"I don't know," Erinn mumbled into her hands. "I really don't know much about her work, but she did mention a recent case that had got under her skin, a violent partner, I think. You'd be better asking her work colleagues, and she's got a home office down the corridor, her password is always Oliver's birthday. August tenth, and he's two."

EIGHT

"DO WE KNOW ANYTHING ABOUT OLIVER?" ANNIE asked Swift as they left Erinn alone in the sitting room and made their way down the long corridor to Jessica's office.

They passed the kitchen, a high-ceilinged room full of dark cupboards and metal appliances, and what must have been Oliver's room with its low bed and toy box. Everywhere was immaculate.

"Here we go," Swift said, opening the door at the far end of the corridor.

The room was as colourful as the rest of the apartment. Truthfully not an office, though, as Jessica's huge bed took up most of the floor space. A small desk stood under the window, neat and tidy, closed drawers tucked underneath.

"The family?" Annie asked, picking up a framed photo from the desk and facing it towards Swift. "Bit weird don't you think? Why not a picture of just

Jessica and Oliver? Why keep the mug of your ex on your work desk?"

Swift took the picture carefully from Annie and studied it. "Perhaps she used his *mug* as incentive to nail the bastards she was prosecuting."

Annie scoffed. "Maybe." She booted up the computer and waited for the password screen to appear.

Swift knelt down beside her and started opening the desk drawers. They put Annie's filing system to shame. They even put the staff filing system to shame. Jessica was organised, neat, and competent.

"This woman seems to have it all," Swift said, whistling through his teeth. "Looks, money, lovely home, family, great job."

"Likely target, you mean?" Annie asked as the computer waited patiently for the password.

"I don't know," Swift replied, his knees clicking as he moved to the next drawer. "I'd have said that would have reduced her likelihood as a target. Intelligent, careful, looks like she has control over her life."

"Deliberately targeted then?" Annie asked, typing in Oliver's date of birth.

Swift pushed himself upright, groaning. "Or the exact opposite, maybe Jessica was in the wrong place at the wrong time?"

"I don't know, this is so meticulously planned that doesn't sit right with me." The computer sprang to life. "From the explosive vest in the first place, that takes a lot of time and skill to prepare. There's the mobile he's using to stay in contact. The way he's setting up each task for Jessica to do. It just feels more prepared than for him to just whip any old Tom, Dick, or Harry off the scene."

Swift made a humming noise and went to check Jessica's bedside table. A lot can be gleaned by what people keep close at hand when they're at their most comfortable. Annie turned her attention back to the computer. The folders were as neat and organised as the apartment. No extraneous files littered the desktop which increased Annie's insecurities about her own. She clicked on the blue documents folder in the bottom right hand of the screen and opened the window. There was a file for every aspect of Jessica's life. Annie picked her work and double clicked to open it.

"I think we're going to need to get tech on this," she called over to Swift. "There are literally hundreds of files. Case numbers, by the looks of it."

Swift looked over, his phone in his hands.

"We're going to need to get someone else on it, tech or no tech," he said, pocketing his phone and heading for the door. "Jessica is on the move again, and she's walking fast."

Annie felt her stomach leap into her chest, she scrambled up from the desk chair and followed Swift back down the corridor to where Erinn sat as still as one of the sculptures.

"Thank you for your time," Swift said. "We have to go now, but we're sending a team of uniformed officers to come and give the place a sweep. Will you be here for the next few hours?"

"I can be," Erinn replied, eyes wide. "Has something happened with Jess?"

"We'll be in touch." Swift was halfway to the door before he'd finished speaking.

"Try not to worry, Erinn," Annie said, quickly. "We're doing our best to keep Jessica safe."

Erinn looked down at her feet, her cheeks stained pink with emotion. "You can try all you want. But until I see her with my own eyes, I'm going to worry"

It was a fair point. Annie gave her that. But there was no time for more empty words of comfort as Swift was holding the door open and giving Annie the look she knew so well.

"What's up?" she asked as they skipped down the stairs and out the door to Swift's car.

Swift hit the button to unlock the 4x4 and he was three point turning around the road before Annie's seat belt was properly fastened.

"Jessica is making her way to the scrubland behind the industrial park at the back of the airport." Swift chicaned in between the parked cars and out onto the main road, narrowly missing a bus as he swung around the corner.

"Crap," Annie wheezed, clinging onto the handle above the door for dear life.

"Yep."

There was two obvious reasons Annie could think of, as to why Jessica was heading where she was heading. The airport, prime target for an explosive device, was she heading there to take down a plane on the tarmac? Was this whole charade just a cover so the perp could zone in on one of the many planes that rolled in and out of Norwich airport? Again, something about this didn't make sense as Annie mulled it over. Why would they want to target a plane travelling from a small airport to places such as Amsterdam or Minorca? Surely to make an impact they needed to go bigger, Luton or Stanstead even, but Norwich? Blowing up a plane in a small airport wasn't making an impact on anyone except the poor families directly involved.

Annie didn't want to think about the second reason Jessica could be heading for scrubland. She either knew she was about to die, that the man contacting her on the mobile had told her to go there and prepare for the worst. Or she was going somewhere uninhabited and far enough away from people to trigger the explosive herself.

"Can you go any faster?" Annie squealed as they bumped down one of the few hills in Norwich and skidded off to a road to their left.

"Not it you want to make it in one piece." Swift had his bottom lip firmly trapped between his teeth, the concentration on his face was laser focussed.

Annie held on and tried not to count the seconds away as they sped along the city roads towards the airport. Nearly three hundred later, Swift tucked the car into a lay-by and killed the engine.

"We still can't get too close," he said to Annie, whose knuckles were so white she was having difficulty unclenching her hand from around the handle. "We don't know if there are eyes on Jessica. Can you pinpoint her exact location?"

Crunching her hands free and getting out her phone, Annie flicked the screens to the Find Me app, her fingers aching.

"There." She tilted the screen to Swift. "She's just the other side of that hedge."

"Okay," he said, pulling his own phone from his pocket. "I can't believe I'm about to say this to you, but I need you to get out there and see if you can talk to Jessica. I'll get on the phone to the airport and check all flights. We'll close the airport if we need to. Just find out what you can."

A small bead of sweat formed on the strip of skin where Swift's hair met his forehead. Annie wanted to take away his stress, somehow, the psychotherapist in her wrestling to get out and help him. But the police officer in her was winning.

"I'll do my best," she said, opening the door as quietly as she could and stepping down into the drizzle.

"Annie?" Swift had shifted in his seat to face her, his eyes searching her face.

Annie tried to swallow but a great lump of fear was blocking the way.

"Yes?" she croaked.

"Please be careful."

"Careful is my middle name." Annie almost laughed. From broken ankles, to nearly getting drowned in a cave, to being moments away from being injected with bubonic plague, being careful was very low on Annie's list of traits.

Swift gave her a wry smile and drew his lips between his teeth, zipping an imaginary zipper across them for good measure. Annie gave him a grin and shut the car door, wishing she could get back in and carry-on winding Swift up. Out here in the cold and the damp, the idea of approaching Jessica when she was possibly ready to set the bomb off was all too real. Annie blew out her cheeks and pulled up the hood of her coat.

The scrubland was vast and eerily quiet. Keeping to the safe side of the metal gate, Annie strained her neck to see into all the corners of the weedy rubble and failed. Instead, she grabbed hold of the top bar and climbed over, her fingers stinging under the cold of the metal. Jumping down onto the scrubland, Annie could see Jessica at the far side, next to the hedge where Swift was parked. It was so high and over-grown, there was no way Jessica could have seen their car, but she would have heard it. Annie fumbled with her phone in her pocket, numb fingers swiping the screen to attempt to send Swift a message.

Move the car, just in case.

She wrote as little as possible, not having the

patience to type anything more, she just needed Swift out of the way of any impending explosions before she made a move towards Jessica.

The woman was too far away for Annie to make out clearly. But even so, from where she was standing by the gate, Annie could see that Jessica was bent double, her face near a thatch of stinging nettles growing from under the hedge.

What is she doing? Praying. Preparing to die.

Annie picked her feet and made her way carefully across the terrain towards her. It was rough underfoot. Annie had no idea what used to stand on the now derelict land, but her guess was a brick building, the rubble ground into the mud and grass when it toppled. She took care over every step; though her instinct was to run towards Jessica, she didn't want to turn her ankle.

"Jessica." Annie shouted when she was close enough for the other woman to hear her. "Jessica, wait."

Jessica startled, the arm that was holding her up off the ground buckled underneath her and she fell face first into the thatch of stingers.

"Ow," Jessica cried, throwing herself back onto her ankles. "Annie? What are you doing here? How did you even know *I* was here?"

Annie skipped the last few metres and came to a stop by Jessica. The young woman's face was beginning to welt, her eyes scrunched against the pain, but underneath the immediate sting of the nettles was a steely look of annoyance.

"Jessica," Annie said, panting, her heart thrumming rapidly in her throat. "There must be some other way, please don't do this. Come with me, we can work something out. Was this your next task? What has he asked you to do?"

Jessica struggled to her feet; the heavy vest hidden under her coat must have been weighing her down.

"Annie," Jessica started, her face twisted. "What do you mean?"

Annie looked up as a plane roared overhead, it was low enough to see faces at the window as they took off on an adventure.

"We're shutting down the airport," she said, nodding upwards. "But we need time. Please give us time."

"What?" Jessica looked up at the plane and then back down at Annie, her eyes as wide as saucers. "Oh no."

NINE

WHAT'S NEW PUSSYCAT

Jessica covered her face in her hands, her whole body shaking, as the plane's wings rattled and the gears folded away above their heads. Annie went to comfort her, a hand on her shoulder, offering words of solace.

"Annie," Jessica rubbed at her face, taking her hands away to reveal the rash of the nettles. White spots littered one cheek and made a string of pearls up to her forehead. "I'm not here to blow up a plane."

Annie took her hands away from Jessica's shoulders and she stood right in front of her, lowering her face so their eyes were level.

"Then, whatever it is, we can figure it out," Annie said, softly. "You don't need to do this. There are ways out of this situation, other than triggering the explosion."

Jessica rolled her eyes. "Look Annie," she said. "I know you're trying to help, but you're doing the exact opposite right now. He doesn't even know I'm here."

Annie squinted against the sun peeking out from behind the rain clouds. Steam rose from the ground where the dampness was evaporating. There was a word for it, the smell of the ground after heavy rain. Annie couldn't remember what the word was, but the smell was all consuming. A new lease of life. Fresh starts.

"Talk to me," she said, stepping away from Jessica and noticing something under the hedge where she had been bending. "What's going on?"

Jessica squatted down and lifted what looked like a metal trap out from under the nettles. It was a large trap, the kind that Annie had used to humanely trap mice when she'd had them in her office because they took a liking to her leftover pizza crusts, but this was much bigger. Jessica propped open the trap door and wiggled it back under the hedge. Ducking her hands in her pockets, Jessica pulled out a packet of Dreamies and dropped some at the back of the cage, making a pursing noise with her lips.

She sat back and motioned for Annie to do the same. The ground was still soaking, but Annie dropped down and sat motionless with Jessica, both of them staring in the direction of the trap stuck under the hedge.

"What's going on?" Annie whispered. "What're you trying to catch?"

"He told me to steal a cat," Jessica whispered back. "To take a family pet and carry it home with me."

"What?" Annie hissed. "That's weird."

"Tell me about it." Jessica kept very still while she was talking. "But I couldn't do it. Graffiti, that's fair game, I felt bad for the person who had to clean it up, but it's not hurting anyone. The pies were harder, I had no idea what was in that syringe. But when I knew your officers were there and that they'd take away the ones I injected, I felt better about it. But this? No way. I'm not going to steal someone's beloved family pet. I've known the devastation of losing a pet and what that does to a family. Especially children."

"That's brutal," Annie agreed, the urge to scratch her itchy nose was tremendous, but she kept her arms still.

"It was the devastation that reminded me of this place, actually," Jessica went on. "I put someone away about a year ago, Luke Hart. I'd forgotten all about him until I got the voice note about the cat."

"Luke Hart?" Annie prompted.

"He would come here and trap strays," she went on. "Keep them in the back of his van while he wrapped their poor little bodies with fireworks. You can guess the rest."

Annie didn't want to.

"Anyway," Jessica continued. "He soon moved from stray cats to people's pets. Dogs, cats, there was even a horse. I was so glad when the jury found him guilty and sentenced him to prison time. He was a horrible piece of work."

Annie chiselled the name Luke Hart into her memory.

"Do you think he could be behind this?" Annie asked. "Explosives, cats, could he be getting to you from inside?"

Jessica sighed. "I did wonder that myself, just this morning when I received this stupid task. But I don't know. Why do this to me?"

"Revenge?"

A rustle in the hedge had both women holding their breath. The silence that followed hurt Annie's ears so much she wanted to swallow and pop it away. But then came the rustling again. There was definitely something in there. Something sniffing out the cat treats. Annie hoped it wasn't a rat. She didn't mind rats, but she wouldn't want to be wrestling a wild one from a trap when she couldn't remember the last time she'd had a tetanus jab. She was wondering if rats carried rabies when the trap snapped shut and an almighty yowl pierced through the air. Nope, definitely a cat.

Jessica pitched forwards and grabbed the handle of the cage, lifting it and making sure the door was firmly shut. A huge pair of green eyes stared through the metal at Annie, she could tell the cat was angry by the way it was looking at her, despite it now being deathly quiet. Jessica pursed her lips at the cage, trying to comfort the creature, but it was shaking and scared and, now Annie could get a good look at it, really rather huge. Matted fur pushed up against the cage, sprouts of it sticking out like wire brush, and the stench coming away from the cage made Annie's eyes water.

"How do you have to prove that you've done this task?" she asked, a finger tipped under her nose to try and stave off the smell.

Jessica lifted the cage to eye level, her arm shaking under the weight. She twisted it slowly round and round to get a good view of the cat from all angles.

"I've got to take a photo of me and the cat at home." Jessica's face was scrunched. "Do you think I should put it back and wait for another one? A less smelly one?"

"No!" Annie was growing fond of the marmalade-coloured cat with its once white bib and wobbly tail. "I mean, you probably don't have time to wait around for another one, do you?"

Her mind flicked back to the explosive strapped to Jessica's chest and the thoughts of fluffy kitties were soon replaced once again with trepidation. And soon after, with Swift.

"Whoops," Annie continued, hoping Swift hadn't gotten as far as closing the airport. She pushed herself up to her feet, her knees clicking, her sore ankle

84

aching in the cold, and grabbed her phone from her pocket, dialling her boss. "Swift? Stand down. No immediate threat."

Annie realised she was talking like an idiot and shook out her shoulders.

"Annie?" Swift replied, his voice muffled as though he was holding the phone over the speaker. "What's going on? I've been worried about you."

"Sorry," she said, watching as Jessica put the cat down and stand up, stretching out her back and lifting her arms to the sky. "Bit of a strange one, this. We've captured a cat. Heading to Jessica's apartment to take a photo of it."

Annie heard Swift snort on the other end of the phone. "This is no time to be Instagramming pictures of a cat, O'Malley, no matter how cute it is. Is it cute?"

"Very," Annie replied. "But, as requested by our, yet unknown, perp. Jessica had to steal a pet, and prove it by sending a photo. Oh, that reminds me. Can you do a search on a Luke Hart, known for explosives and for cat... GBH?"

"On it," Swift said. "And Annie, do you think it's a good idea that Jessica goes back to her apartment, her sister is still there? We could be putting her at risk."

Annie had wondered this herself. But there was no way of knowing if the perp knew what Jessica's apartment looked like and if they'd spot that she was taking the photo somewhere else.

"I think we're going to have to risk it, Swift," she said. "I'll go back with Jessica, I think she'll need some help with the cage, can you pick up some cat cleaning stuff on your way? Meet you there."

"Stuff to clean a cat, or stuff to clean up after a cat?" Swift asked, laughing.

Jessica picked up the cage and held it at arm's length as the cat swiped with outstretched claws at Jessica's torso. Annie quickly pealed the cage from Jessica's hands, not wanting a stray cat paw to be the trigger for the explosive that, up until now, was thankfully dormant. She almost gagged, the smell of rotting flesh more pungent now the cat was free of the shield of the hedge. It hissed at her, a low throaty growl, and its breath was almost as bad.

"Both," Annie replied to Swift, and ended the call, turning to Jessica she went on. "I'm coming to yours; we'll need to get the kitty cleaned up as best we can before you take a picture. This does not look like a family pet unless it's come directly from the Addams Family."

"Sunday Addams," Jessica laughed. "It is Sunday, isn't it?"

"Not yet, it's still Saturday, but I like that name," Annie replied, heading back towards the gate, the cage wobbling in her hands as the cat lost its balance. "Where's your car?"

"I'm not keeping the cat, you know?" Jessica sped up and overtook Annie, heading for the far end of the scrubland beyond the gate Annie had climbed over. "So, there's really no point naming it."

Out of sight of Jessica, Annie lifted the cage a little higher to whisper to Sunday. "It's okay, puss puss, she'll come around, I'm sure you'll be friendly with a little love and attention."

Sunday's green eyes darkened with his dilating pupils and a grubby paw, claws extended, shot out of the cage, and swiped Annie right on the chin.

TEN

"WHAT THE HELL IS THAT?" SWIFT CRIED FROM THE safety of the doorway to Jessica's bathroom.

Annie jumped, trying to look at Swift, while still holding down a feral cat who was fighting for its life in a bathtub with a thimble full of lukewarm water.

"This is Sunday," Annie said, gripping tighter as the cat wriggled under her skiing gloves.

She'd had to borrow the gloves from Jessica to keep the skin on her hands intact. Sunday didn't like the bath; he didn't like much it would seem. But the water had rendered him rather pathetic looking, a skinny little thing with drooping hair and ears too large for his head. Annie's heart strings were being well and truly tugged.

Swift knelt down next to Annie and dropped a carrier bag at his knees.

"Cat stuff," he said, nodding at the bag.

"Great, thanks," Annie said. "Can you pour him some bubble bath?"

Jessica appeared at the door, keeping well away from the splashing in case it damaged the wiring on the explosive vest.

"Sorry I can't help," she said, quietly, slipping back out of the bathroom before she'd even really arrived.

Now she was home, Jessica looked like she could lay down on her bed and sleep for a week. Annie had taken a video of the whole device and sent it to their tech team to see if it was safe to remove while they waited for the EOD. Erinn had put the kettle on and whipped up some food for her sister, but Jessica's tiredness looked bone deep and unshakable while she was still strapped up in a life-threatening corset. Erinn had been thrown, not quite sure how to handle the fragility of her older sister. The younger woman was keeping her distance and eyeing her sister warily like she was a stray dog who could attack at any moment.

Sunday flipped around under Annie's hands, his legs thrashing at the sides of the bath. He couldn't get purchase, but Annie wasn't about to let him go. She'd found the source of the smell, a large abscess on Sunday's neck had burst and matted his fur together with a thick gooey liquid. Annie knew he needed antibiotics to treat it but getting the cat clean and warm and fed was her priority, the vets weren't open this late, and she'd send Swift out with his wallet to an out of hours practice once they'd taken Sunday's picture.

"Any news from the station?" Annie asked.

Swift lifted a bottle from the carrier bag and unscrewed the lid, tipping an oddly bitter scented liquid into the water. Sunday was thrashing around so erratically, he was lathering up the bubbles nicely, so Annie just let him get on with it. The water splashed up her arms and over her jumper, creating a damp patch on the floor by her knees. She hoped the cat would appreciate the effort when he was warm and dry and had a full belly, but somehow, she doubted it.

"Nothing on Luke Hart yet, but the tech team have been working on locating a trace on the mobile," Swift said, drifting his hand along the top of the water. Sunday took a swipe at him and he quickly retreated. "It looks like it's a burner. They've been studying the photo you took and the video you just sent them and think they know a little more about the explosive though."

"Oh yeah?" Annie glanced at Swift.

Swift looked over his shoulder towards the bathroom door and the corridor outside. He pushed himself to his feet and quietly clicked the door shut. Dropping the lid on the toilet he took a seat and puffed out his cheeks. Annie did not like the look on his face.

"The team have been studying the photo and video you sent them, good work on that idea, by the way," Swift said in almost a whisper.

"Swift," Annie interrupted, Sunday causing a tsunami of water to cascade over the edge of the bath. "You're going to have to speak up a bit, I can't hear you over Nessie here."

Swift grabbed a towel from the heated rail and in a movement so quick Annie didn't see him coming, he swooped into the bath with it and scooped out a cleanish Sunday. The cat looked straggly, thin as a rake, wrapped in the towel, but he'd stopped scratching. Swift looped the towel around Sunday's body a few times and held him close lying in his lap as he took his seat back on the toilet lid. Annie marvelled at the way Sunday was looking up at Swift, his big green eyes round, dark, like Puss in Boots when he's after some food.

"That's not fair," she said, pushing herself up on the side of the bath and perching on the edge. "I do all the hard work and you come in and he's all purring and lovely."

"Animals love me," Swift said, shrugging.

Annie raised an eyebrow. "Well there's no accounting for taste," she mocked, kindly.

"Anyway," Swift went on. "The tech team are almost one hundred per cent sure it's a real explosive. The wires are professionally strapped up, the material of the vest looks like it's one that could have been military grade, though they're not sure about that and those kinds of vests are easy to get hold of these days. It's just tightly woven material with a load of pockets."

"Why does it have to be tightly woven?" Annie asked, the sound of purring filling the room.

"This is the most worrying part," Swift went on. "You mentioned to the EOD that Jessica said the vest was heavy, yes?"

Annie nodded.

"The pipe bombs that are used in these kinds of vests aren't that weighty." Swift shifted Sunday in his arms so he had a free hand to tickle under his chin.

"What does that mean?" Annie asked.

"That the vest is more than likely strapped with shrapnel too."

Annie sighed. "And what's the consequence of the vest being loaded with shrapnel as well as explosives?"

"Depending on what kind of items have been used, and we're talking ball bearings, nails, screws, wires, all sorts really," Swift said, grimly, "the radius of the explosion becomes wider and more lethal. Maybe fifteen metres with damage possible in a three-hundred-and-sixty-degree circumference."

"So not just injuring Jessica," Annie added. "But anyone near to her too? With deadly force?"

Swift nodded.

"Great," Annie felt dejected, she had been hoping the device was a well-made fake. "Any good news?"

Swift slowly started to open the towel, inspecting the wound on Sunday's neck. Now it was clean, Annie could see it was as large as a golf ball and just as spherical.

"The tech team have sourced the footage from the CCTV of the courts," Swift said, drying Sunday's fur as gently as if the cat was a baby. "There's footage of Jessica leaving the courts, she's alone and there's no sign of anyone else in the minutes immediately before or after. But the cameras that look out over the gardens at the front, the ones which would show the road too, nothing."

"Nothing?" Annie prompted. "She's alone again?"

Swift shook his head. "Literally nothing, they weren't working."

"That's coincidental." Annie scrunched her forehead. "Who owns those cameras?"

"The courts do," Swift replied, Sunday starting to look like a giant fluff ball in his lap. "They own them all, inside and out. They even own the ones looking over the pavement as they're attached to the court walls."

"Crap," Annie sighed. "What about the car park?"

"We're waiting on a warrant for those."

"What?" Annie couldn't hide her shock. "Do they know about the bomb?"

"Yup," Swift replied. "Makes you wonder what they're hiding that's more dodgy than an explosive."

"Jeez," Annie said. "How long before that comes back?"

"Monday at the earliest, the judge doesn't work on the weekends," Swift raised an eyebrow and Annie agreed with the sentiment.

"Ironic," she whispered.

"What do you think?" Swift asked, as Annie was chewing the inside of her lip, staring at the murky water stagnant in the bathtub.

"I think that it is sounding more likely that Jessica was our target," Annie said, her eyes transfixed on a group of sticky burrs floating in a circle on the water. "The location, the timing, the way it's been carried out. With the addition of the broken CCTV, it's looking like the whole thing was planned down to the very last minute, and Jessica wasn't just in the wrong place at the wrong time, she was exactly who they were after."

"Agreed," said Swift. "But that wasn't what I was asking for your opinion on. What do you think of Sunday?"

Swift released the towel from around the cat, who stayed laying in his lap. His fur was clean and drying, sticking up like Annie's did in the mornings. His eyes looked brighter, his wound looked manageable, and though there were still matted patches all over his little body, Sunday had scrubbed up a treat.

"He's like a different cat," Annie said, leaning over and raising a hand to tickle behind his head.

Sunday blanched, his ears flattening, his throaty growl returning. Swift chuckled as the cat stood up and stretched out his legs, circling and sitting back on Swift's knee as though he belonged there.

"Er, that's uncalled for mister," Annie said, softly, leaving Sunday to his snoozes. "Shall I go and get Jessica? We need to get this photo taken asap."

"I'll stay here," Swift said with a smile. "Wouldn't want to disturb the star of the moment. Let the water out of the bath, would you O'Malley? It stinks."

Annie drew up her sleeve and pulled out the plug, watching the dirt and pus circle the drain. She shuddered and ran her arm under the sink tap, thoroughly washing her hands with an exuberant amount of soap. As she scrubbed away with the only dry towel left in the bathroom, the doorbell rang out. Annie kept motionless, looking to Swift for advice.

"You go," he said, reading her face. "Don't let anyone else answer it, or anyone else in."

With a quick nod, Annie opened the bathroom door and sped down the hallway. Jessica and Erinn hovered by the living room door, looking as unsure as Annie had been.

"Get back inside the room," she whispered. "I'll deal with whoever it is."

Pulling her shoulders back, Annie unlocked the door and drew it open, noticing too late just how dishevelled she looked covered in water and cat fur.

"Can I help you?" she asked, smiling as widely as she could.

The caller was a man, early forties, well dressed in clothes that looked relaxed enough for a weekend, but expensive enough to still look good. He had a dusting of grey hair in a dark, neat beard and eyes that looked as though they'd snared a few women in their time.

"I'm sure you can," he said, with a grin that confirmed Annie's suspicions. He leant casually against the door frame, peeking past Annie to the hallway. "I'm after Jessica."

"She's not here at the moment," Annie replied, willing the sisters to stay quiet. "Can I take a message?"

"I'm sure you can," he said, again. "I'm Dylan Burrows, esquire, LLB, LLM, FLBA member. I work with Jessica and need to talk to her quite urgently about a case. Why don't you tell me your name, we've not met before, I'd definitely remember?"

"I'll pass it on," Annie replied, stiffly. "Does she have your number?"

Dylan Burrows was obviously not used to being snubbed. Wrong footed, he opened and closed his mouth like a goldfish before nodding.

"Good," Annie said, hoping to close the conversation. "I'll let her know you came over."

Annie stepped back from the door, encouraging Dylan to do the same, but something had caught his attention over Annie's shoulder.

"Nice cat," he said, smirking. "New addition?"

Annie turned and caught a wash of ginger as Sunday sped across the hallway. She pushed the door shut as quickly as she could, not wanting the cat to escape, bashing Dylan in the arm as she did.

"Right, I see how it is," she heard Dylan through the closed door. "Can you let Jessica know she needs to answer her calls and emails. The jury made their decision pretty quickly about Henry Chance and she needs to be back in court to hear it or they can't proceed. Tell her to stop slacking and pull her finger out. And tell her the new addition to the family is as pretty as a picture."

Annie drew breath, she was fed up with Dylan and his sleazy ways already. Even with a closed door between them.

"Though it's a weird addition because I know she hates cats," Dylan shouted and Annie could hear the smugness on his face as he said it and wished she could slam the door in his face all over again.

ELEVEN

With the footsteps of Dylan Burrows echoing away down the corridor, Annie turned her attention back to Jessica's apartment and the chaos ensuing behind her. Sunday's deep growls rolled across the wooden floors, emanating from the living room. She could hear Swift making kissy noises, hopefully aimed at the cat, and Jessica and Erinn laughing. The sounds were a tonic from the stressful twenty-four hours since Annie and Swift were pulled away from the retirement party. Clicking the door locked, Annie went to see what was going on.

The living room was much as she remembered it from their visit with Erinn, but it looked as though it had been hit with a tornado in the meantime. The rugs were all askew, cushions had been thrown from the chairs, and some of the ornaments Annie had been admiring, were now in pieces on the herringbone. Jessica and Erinn huddled together on the smaller of the sofas, smiles on their tired faces. Annie blanched when she saw their proximity along with the information Swift had given her about the explosive but didn't want to say anything for fear of sudden movements. She looked around for Swift, who was by the window, gazing up towards the ceiling light.

"Everything okay?" she asked, drawing out her words.

"No, it's not bloody okay," Swift hissed like he had been taking tips from Sunday. "Look at him."

He pointed up to the light fitting and there, as calm as anything, was Sunday, peering down from the scooped light shade with what Annie could have sworn was a grin on his face.

"Hello Sunday," she said, edging to the middle of the room where the fitting hung. "How did you get all the way up there, you silly cat?"

Swift cleared his throat behind her.

"He used the living room as his own death bike cage, but without the bike," he said, and Jessica and Erinn laughed again. "Then when he couldn't go round and round anymore, he mounted the painting, scrambled up to the top, and took the leap of faith."

Annie looked to where Swift was pointing. It was the haphazardly painted artwork Swift had valued at over thirty thousand earlier. She walked up to it, noticing plucks in the canvas, scrapes in the paint, and one tiny wet paw print dabbed into the very top corner.

"He's probably doubled the value," she said,

trying not to laugh. "At least you know he has good taste."

"O'Malley," Swift had his stern, boss-like voice on. "Any ideas how we can get him down to have his picture taken?"

Annie walked back to the window where Swift had the best view of Sunday, pondering for a while as Sunday cleaned his face languorously. The lightshade was copper, domed in a way that made Annie itch with the amount of dust that must collect there. But Sunday was enjoying himself. Out of everyone's way and safe.

"Go and find a tin of tuna or salmon," she said, knowing the best way to get the cat to come down was through his stomach. "Or get a sachet of whatever you brought with you from the shops, and a small plate."

Annie took a seat on the chair beside the sofa where the sisters watched with wide eyes.

"Swift," she shouted after him, noticing a slight shake to Jessica's hands and the paleness of her face. "Get the kettle on and make some milky, sweet tea while you're in there, would you?"

"You've got him well trained," Erinn said, smiling as Swift went about his chores without a word.

"Don't tell anyone," Annie said, leaning in conspiratorially. "But he's most at home in a kitchen, whipping up something delicious to eat. Looks like he feels exactly the same when it's a cat to look after and not just a human."

The girls laughed and Annie felt something squirm in her stomach, a reminder that they were against a clock and a madman.

"Jessica," Annie said, seriously now. "That was a colleague of yours at the door. Dylan Burrows?"

Jessica grunted. "What did he want?"

Annie could tell that Jessica liked Dylan about as much as she did.

"He said that the jury had come to a decision about a Henry, or was it a Harry, Chance?" Annie saw Jessica's mouth drop.

"Already?" The poor woman looked haggard. "I need to get back to work. Henry Chance needs his sentencing; he needs to be off the streets. Nothing can go wrong with this one, he's dangerous."

Erinn took Jessica's hands in her own, her eyes wide.

"Jessica," she said, softly. "You can't go to work, not now. You're too tired, you'll make mistakes. Innocent people might end up locked away because you're not at your best. That's not fair to you or to the people you're prosecuting."

"Don't be stupid." Jessica was short with her sister, the voracity of her words making Annie flinch. "I've already done all the hard work. All that's left is to see the judge's verdict, but I need to be there."

Annie shook her head. "You can't go, not until this is over."

"But that's not going to happen." Jessica looked like a caged animal. "I need to go. I'm up against people like Dylan for my job, and it's twice as hard for a woman to get where I am. If I don't pick up the slack, they'll soon gloss over me. I can't not…"

The energy sapped from Jessica before she had the chance to finish her sentence. Her shoulder slumped and her chin rested on the bulk of vest underneath her coat.

"It's real, isn't it? The bomb." she asked, her red rimmed eyes on Annie.

Annie nodded. "I'm sorry," she said. "It's looking like it is."

"Henry Chance is a piece of work," Jessica said, quietly. "But if Dylan Burrows wants to go and get the credit for my work then I'm going to have to let him, aren't I? He can do the press talks outside the court, whatever, just please don't let Chance go free just because I can't be there."

"We can postpone until Monday," Swift said, coming back from the kitchen laden with a heavy tray of food for Sunday the cat and tea for the humans. "Another day won't hurt, and we'll hope to get you out of this before then."

"What do you mean?" Erinn was staring at her sister. "What's real? Why can't you go, it's not just tiredness is it? What's going on?"

Jessica looked between her sister and the two police officers, pleading with her eyes. Swift gave her a nod and she opened her coat a fraction.

"I've been strapped with explosives," Jessica said. "And I can't get free."

Erinn shot to her feet, backing away into the coffee table. It caught the soft skin at the backs of her knees, buckling her legs from under her and depositing her with a thump on the glass top.

"What the hell," she screamed. "What? Why did nobody tell me?" The younger sister scrabbled back to her feet, her face pink, a sheen of sweat making her glow, she turned to Swift, her mouth twisted. "You. You need to get her out of it. Get it off her. Get it off her now."

She was pacing. Up and down the living room with long strides, her arms tightly clasped around her body.

"Erinn." Annie stood carefully, not wanting to panic the girl more. "You need to stay calm."

"Calm," Erinn interrupted. "Don't tell me to stay calm, my sister is going to die."

The realisation hit with her words, and she dropped to her knees on the floor, head in hands, sobbing.

"My sister is going to die," she said, her words muffled with her fingers and her sobs. "Please help her."

Jessica rose from the sofa and Annie thought she was going to comfort Erinn. She put out an arm to stop her, not wanting Erinn to lash out at Jessica by accident and end the whole thing here and now. But Jessica slipped out of the room and Annie heard a door click shut further down the corridor. She looked to Swift with a raised brow.

"Erinn." Swift knelt beside the younger sister and placed a hand on her curved back. "I promise you we're going to do everything in our power to help Jessica. But we need you to be strong for her too. She needs calmness right now, and stability. We can't afford to make any sudden moves or do anything too physical with Jessica. We're not sure who we're dealing with right now. But they're clever and they're organised, and we need to stay one step ahead. So can you get up for me? You're okay."

Erinn lifted her head from her hands; tears stained her face and her lips and cheeks were puffy from crying.

"I'm sorry," she sniffed. "I'm not sure what came over me."

The young woman unravelled her long limbs and pulled herself back up onto the sofa, chewing the sides of her mouth.

"Whoever it is who is doing this," Annie began as Swift handed Erinn a steaming cup of sugary tea, "is asking Jessica to carry out tasks for him. Our priority is to keep Jessica safe, and those around her safe, and so we really need to get Sunday down from the light and take his photo."

Erinn wiped a hand down her face, stretching her eyes open.

"Jessica took a photo of him earlier," she said. "When he ran in here after his bath."

"What?" Annie shot.

"Yeah," Erinn replied. "I did wonder what on

earth she was doing, but she grabbed him when he ran in and took a picture with her phone. I wondered what she was doing because neither Jessica nor the cat looked very happy about the whole thing."

"So she's already sent it?" Annie was talking to Swift now.

"With me," he said, marching to the hallway.

Annie skipped to keep up, her heart racing. If Jessica had already sent the photo, then the next task could already be in hand. Had Jessica gone out the apartment already? What if the cat was the last task? What if there was nothing, now, between them all and a short sharp goodbye? Swift reached Jessica's bedroom and flung open the door.

"Miss Frampton," he called out for her before stepping inside.

Annie wasn't far behind and what greeted them chilled her to the bone.

Jessica had removed her coat and the vest was there in all its glory, a ticking time bomb from every angle.

"Jessica?" Annie was wary, the way Jessica had snubbed her sister and snuck out of the living room didn't fill her with confidence that the woman was doing okay. "Can we come in?"

"You already are, aren't you?" Jessica spat.

"What have you done?" Annie asked, edging slowly towards the bed, Jessica on the other side ready to flee.

"I did what I was told to do," she shouted. "I've

got to do what I was told to do because you are all useless. I'm still trapped in my own body because you haven't worked out how to get me out of this thing."

Jessica pulled at the straps of the vest, violently shaking it back and forth. Annie flinched; her body taut with adrenaline. Swift stepped forward into the room in two large strides and grabbed Jessica's wrists, pulling her hands away from the vest and out to her sides.

"And we won't get a chance to if you keep doing that," he said, sternly. "Please sit down and talk to us."

He let go off Jessica's arms and they dropped gently to her sides. The mattress sank as she sat down, Swift next to her. Jessica fumbled with her phone, handing it to Swift.

"I can't do this anymore," she said, her face still, almost doll like.

Annie was worried about Jessica's mental state, how much longer could the poor woman go on with the stress. Humans weren't designed to carry this level of stress over such long periods of time. The fight or flight response is a quick action, saving mankind from predators so they can run away to safety. This wasn't an animal predator, though, and fight or flight wasn't helping Jessica flee from herself.

"Annie, I think you need to see this." Swift handed her the phone and she glanced at the text message on the screen, bile rising from her empty stomach.

Kill the cat.

TWELVE

Annie sat the cat carrier down on the pavement and fumbled in her bag for her door key. Unlocking the door, she lifted the carrier, Sunday's dead weight was not moving, not shifting around and unbalancing her as he had been when she'd carried his cage to Jessica's car from the shrubland where they'd caught him. She hoisted him up higher and made kissy noises, though she knew he couldn't hear her.

Her flat was warm where the sun had been streaming in all day through the opened blinds. Placing the cage delicately on the desk, Annie went over to the kitchenette and filled the kettle. She could have murdered a glass of red wine, but Swift had told her to be back in the office by seven, even though tomorrow was a Sunday and it was already nearly midnight.

She let the water run for a moment, running her hands under the stream, feeling the weight of the last few days sloshing off her skin and down the plughole. They'd left Jessica with Erinn, safe in the knowledge that she'd sent proof of the latest task.

The last text Jessica had received had been to sleep because tomorrow was a new day, whatever the hell he'd meant by that. Annie hadn't wanted to leave Sunday at Jessica's because it was obvious she wasn't keen on cats and Annie had developed a friendship with him, albeit a very one-sided, non-reciprocal friendship. Besides, Jessica could have been Snow White on a normal day, singing with her animal friends, but the position she found herself in would render anyone unable to focus on anything but the tasks in hand.

Annie put the kettle under the tap, her fingers now numb with the cold from the water. Filling it, she set it to boil, her arms aching and weary, her heart heavy. It was weird to think that it was only just over twenty-four hours since Annie had first met Jessica, and now here she was with a list of question in her head and a cat carrier on her desk. She looked over at it, wondering what on earth she was going to do with Sunday now when the carrier tilted slightly to one side, a shuffling noise emanating from inside.

"Sunday?" Annie sang, heading to her desk, and dropping heavily into her chair. "Wakey, wakey sleepyhead."

She poked a finger in the bars of the cage and was greeted with a low growl and a quick swipe with retracted claws.

"We're getting somewhere," Annie laughed, lifting the cage to the floor, and unlocking the door. "You make yourself at home, and I'll sort out your stuff, can't have you weeing in the pot plant now, can we?"

Sunday wobbled out of his cage and headed straight for the plant on Annie's windowsill. Up until this moment, the plant had been Annie's only pet, now she had a grumpy old cat to deal with too.

The vet had made an emergency call to Jessica's flat. And while the young woman and her sister had been hidden away in Jessica's bedroom, Annie and Swift had played happy families, pretending that Sunday had been in a fight and that's why he was injured and hiding on the ceiling. Luckily the vet had managed to calm him enough to come down and be given a high dose of antibiotics and a hearty sedative. So much so that he'd collapsed in a heap on his side, so soundly asleep he was snoring, probably for the first time in his whole feline life. They'd thanked the vet with an extortionate amount of money that Swift swore he'd claim back from the office and taken a quick photo in which he looked as dead as the proverbial Dodo.

"There we go," Annie said, setting out his food bowl in the kitchen area and his litter tray out in the lobby.

She was planning on moving it up to the small bathroom in the morning, but she didn't want any accidents today, not when she was running on fumes.

Setting up his water fountain by the pot plant, Annie grabbed her camomile tea and pulled out her camp bed, throwing off her clothes and falling into a sleep almost as soon as her head hit the pillow.

At some point between then and the sun rising, Sunday found a cosy spot on Annie's pillow and circled a few times before plonking himself down unceremoniously on Annie's head.

SUNDAY

"Everything alright, O'Malley?" Page was dishing out the pastries in the incident room when Annie pushed through the door, her hand holding her neck in the only position it didn't scream in pain.

"I'll be fine," she replied, taking a seat, and grabbing a pain au chocolat. "I've got a heated pad in my bag, it's less painful when it's warm. I just couldn't balance it and walk at the same time."

She bent tentatively and pulled out the wheat sack she'd microwaved in the staff canteen on her way through. The heat softened the sharp pain, but the aching was deeper.

"Bloody cat," she added, as Swift and Tink arrived.

"Morning," Swift boomed. "Thanks for coming in so early on a Sunday. Oh, Annie, how is the little tyke?"

"Slept on my pillow and gave me a crook in my neck," Annie said, pointing to the wheat bag. "Ate all his food, poo'd it out just outside his litter tray, then started grooming his backside on my desk."

"Glad to hear he's settled in," Swift laughed, grabbing an apricot and pecan slice. "Right, down to business."

He moved to the front of the room and the blue noticeboard, tacking up a picture of Erinn and Dylan Burrows.

"So yesterday," he began. "Annie and I met Jessica's sister, Erinn." He pointed at her photo, her long black curls and huge green eyes made her look like a Disney Princess. "Tink, can you do a check on her, just in case? She's staying with Jessica for the time being, but she looked scared, so I don't know how long she'll be there for."

"On it," Tink replied, saluting Swift with manicured fingers.

"From the CCTV footage," Swift went on. "It looks as though Jessica was targeted. There's been some tampering with the cameras outside the courts, and we're still bloody waiting for the car park footage, Tink can you chase that up too, please?"

Tink waved, her mouth now full of pastry.

"Page." Swift turned to the young DC. "Any more info on the graffiti? Tox results back from the injected food, yet?"

Page wiped his hands down his trousers and swapped places at the front of the room with Swift.

"The graffiti hasn't turned anything else up," he said. "The paint is available anywhere, there were no prints other than Jessica's on the cans, and the words were Shakespeare, as Tink already pointed out."

"Nothing hidden in the words?" Annie asked. "No clues or acrostics?"

"Not that I, or our tech team could see," Page replied. "Just bog-standard Shakespeare."

"Oh, Page," Tink cried. "If your English teacher could see you now, they'd be having a fit. Bog standard? The bard?"

Page raised an eyebrow at Tink, "if my English teacher could see me now, she'd be having a fit that I've got a good job and I'm not locked away myself." Swift cleared his throat. "And I obviously declared all of that in my application," Page added, quickly, his cheeks reddening. "Anyway, moving on. The tox results have come back and the pies were laced with alpha-methylphenethylamine."

"Amphetamines?" Swift's brow creased. "So, the perp just wanted the pie eaters to, what, have a good time?"

"Yeah," Page went on. "But get this. There were also traces of propanamide."

Swift stood abruptly; his palms flat on the table. "Fentanyl? How much?"

"Three hundred micrograms," Page said, looking down at a printout on the desk in front of him. "Not lethal, but pretty strong."

Swift ran his hands through his hair, puffing out his cheeks. He moved back to the front of the room and wrote out the drug names on the white board, circling a question mark beside them.

"If we hadn't known about the laced pies then we could have had very poorly people." Swift turned back to look at his team. "At that time of night and with those types of foods, it's likely that someone who's already taken something may have ingested the fentanyl and the amphetamine, causing catastrophic reactions."

"So, you're saying the pies *were* designed to kill?" Annie felt her heart sink.

"Not necessarily," Swift went on. "But they had the potential to. Right now we don't know whether the perp knew about the potential for fatalities or not."

"We don't even know if they knew the amphetamine was laced," Tink added, pursing her lips.

"Good point, Tink," Swift nodded at her. "Page, can you check whether there have been any other batches of amphetamine laced with fentanyl recently? Any deaths, any seized drugs, anything you can find?"

"Sir," Page said, jotting something down in his notebook. "There were four pies laced in total, so not huge numbers."

"We only need one of those to be eaten by the wrong person and that's one too many," Swift said.

"Yeah," Page went on. "But if this was about mass casualties then the whole shop could have been targeted, or they could have been laced with a lethal dose."

Swift sucked at his teeth. Annie glanced out the window at the rising sun, her brain whirring with the new information.

"It's almost as though we're being given a warning," she said, eyes still focussed out at the trees. "It doesn't feel like Jessica is being asked to do anything really dangerous. Not yet, anyway. What were they, the warm up?"

"Poor old Sunday would disagree," Swift said, the corners of his mouth lifting.

"Sunday?" Tink asked, sipping from her water bottle.

"O'Malley rescued the cat from certain death," Swift replied. "The next task was to kill the cat Jessica had stolen. Annie had already named it at this point so there was no way that was going to happen."

"Don't act like you would have let it happen even if he wasn't called Sunday," Annie said, her attention back in the room now. "You loved it more than I did."

"I didn't take it home with me,'" Swift said.

"You said we should drop it at a rescue centre," Annie smiled, knowing full well Swift would never have done that.

"Alright you two," Tink piped up. "You can continue this argument outside of work hours. For now, I've got some interesting information from Jessica's caseload."

Swift motioned for Tink to take the floor.

"Jessica has put away a lot of criminals, she's good at her job," Tink said, tacking three more pictures to the boards, arrest photos replete with height markers and date boards. "There are a lot of homicide, GBH, ABH, and drugs. This guy here is Henry Chance, most recent defendant, awaiting the results of the jury as I understand." Tink pointed at the photo of a well-dressed, young man. Suave, suited, and seemingly in control. "I also looked at any with markers from the case we're working on now; explosives, animal cruelty, drugs, and we whittled it down to one in particular, this guy here, Luke Hart."

Tink pointed to the photo of a young man, shaven head, crazy eyes, wide smile for the camera.

"Jessica mentioned Luke too," Annie told the room. "When she was trapping Sunday, it was his case that gave her the idea of trapping a stray and not stealing someone's pet."

"He's got a long rap sheet which includes all of the above and get this." Tink tapped finger on the final photo of another young man, dark hair, almost black eyes, jaw as chiselled as Superman. "This is Alfie Leek, Luke Hart's cellmate, and he's requested our company. Apparently, he's got something to tell us."

THIRTEEN

ANNIE HAD NEVER BEEN INSIDE A PRISON. EVEN though prior to working with Swift and the MCU, she had been a member of the probation service, hers had been a post release role seeing probationers in her own office. So it was nothing like she had imagined from her hours of watching crime dramas on the small laptop tucked into her camp bed.

An officer buzzed them through the gate; Annie went first, patted down by the guards with a watchful eye on her from the scary looking dog in the corner. They passed through a metal detector and out into a building that felt very much like the police station. Yellowy blue walls met with squeaky laminate flooring and bright strip lights. The only difference was the intermittent thick metal doors which required a swipe card and a key to open.

They were deposited in a bright, airy room with high, barred windows, and tables and chairs fixed to the floor. It was a large room, enough to feel spacious which Annie was glad of, because being unable to see outside was making her skin itch. She paced the floor, wondering how on earth the prisoners got used to being locked up inside. It was enough to make Annie never even break the speed limit again.

"You okay?" Swift asked, appearing by her side with a calming, warm hand on her arm.

"Not sure I like it in prison," she replied, tugging at the collar of her shirt. "Even if it's only for a few hours on a Sunday."

"That's the general idea," Swift replied, putting an arm around Annie's shoulder, and squeezing.

"But surely the prisoners still have to feel... I don't know, okay with where they are living?" Annie asked, feeling sorry for all the men locked up in the cells beyond the room they were waiting in.

Swift squeezed Annie's shoulder again and went to pull out a chair for her, forgetting it was bolted to the floor.

"Your kindness for all of humanity is what makes you such a wonderful person and friend, O'Malley," he said, smiling.

"And your chivalry knows no bounds," Annie replied, laughing at the chair. "We should probably sit down and look like we know what we're doing. I imagine they're watching us on the cameras, and we don't want them to chuck us out before we've even spoken to... who are we speaking to again?"

"Alfie Leek, cellmate of Luke Hart." Swift took a

breath, about to say more when the lock on the door behind them beeped and clunked and the door swung open to the face of a young man, no older than mid-twenties. Shackled at the hands and dressed in a standard issue grey tracksuit, Annie felt her heart go out to him as the guard pushed him forwards until he dropped into the seat opposite.

"I'll be at the door if you need me," the guard told them before turning to Alfie Leek. "You. Behave."

Alfie grimaced and waved his hands in the air with a hint of *how can I misbehave with these handcuffs?* The guard huffed and slammed the door shut with more gusto than he needed to, the metal reverberating around the room.

"Alfie," Swift began, when the room stilled. "I'm DI Swift, this is Annie O'Malley. I understand you wanted to talk with us?"

Annie watched the young man carefully, wondering how he was coping being incarcerated in this room. He sat as still as a statue, his hands laid gently in his lap, his feet flat on the floor. There was no fidgeting, no tapping of his feet or fingers, nothing. It made Annie relax a little herself.

Alfie would have been as attractive as the picture Tink had shown them, were it not for the yellow pallor of someone who wasn't getting enough sun and vitamins. His hair was almost jet back, dropping into his eyes which made them pop like coal and it was clear he spent his time working out as the tracksuit was bulging at the upper arms and thighs.

"Can I have your assurance that whatever I say won't come back to bite me?" The young man leant forwards, leaning his arms on the table. The handcuffs clunked heavily against the plastic. "I won't talk unless you can make me that promise. You don't know what it's like in here. So make sure I'm safe. Probably the best way to do that is to move me away from Luke, the other wing's got space I hear."

Swift mirrored Alfie's movements, leaning onto the table, his posture open and easy, yet Annie could see the tendons at the side of his neck poised, giving away how tense he really was.

"'We can't make promises like that," Swift said, stoically. "And you know it. So don't mess us around and tell us what it was you wanted to tell us."

Alfie rolled his eyes and slunk back in his seat like a sack of porridge, all his wily ways vacating the room.

"Worth a try, aint it?" he said, shrugging. "I want to move to the other wing, they've got loads more perks and Luke stinks, man. It's rough sharing a bunk."

Annie silently gave Swift his dues, she had been taken in by Alfie and his diminished nature, but now she knew better. She should have known better anyway, given that boys like Alfie had been her work bread and butter for years.

"Talk to us Alfie," Swift sat back in his chair, his arms casually draped. "Or was this just a ploy to get out of your cell for an hour or so?"

Alfie shook his head, his eyes glancing at the door.

"No mate," he said, the handcuffs clattering on the table as the young man scratched an itch on his leg. "It's Luke, man, he's said some stuff that worried me, you know? I just... I'm a bit worried about saying it now we're all here, like."

"What are you inside for?" Annie interjected, changing tact. She had seen this kind of bravado before, it was all a show, and to tattle on someone in prison took a great deal of real bravery.

"Bit of this, bit of that," Alfie shuffled in his seat to direct his answer to Annie.

"Want to narrow that down?" she asked, smiling.

"Threatening with a bladed article in a public place, if you want it's proper name." Archie's face clouded. "I wasn't gonna do anything with it, you know. Just wanted to give them a bit of a scare, that's all."

Swift cleared his throat and crossed his arms over his chest. "It was a Rambo Bowie Tactical Survival knife, wasn't it?" he asked, his voice clipped. "Scary looking things, twelve inches of steel blade with a serrated edge and a dangerous looking curved tip. Correct me if I'm wrong."

Alfie and Swift stared at each other for a moment. The tension in the room thickening as though it was being boiled to a bubbling stew.

"Just because it looked pretty tough." Alfie

couldn't help a smile creep onto his lips. "Didn't mean I was gonna use it."

"Who were you scaring?" Annie asked, trying not to show her discomfort at the rise in temperature in the room.

Alfie shrugged, hunching in his chair, his chin nearly hitting his chest. "They'd been warned already about being on our turf. I needed to step it up a notch."

"Drugs?" Swift asked.

"I don't touch the things." Alfie didn't break his stare from Swift. "They killed my brother. They're the devil's work."

"Talk to us about Luke," Annie asked, pointedly. They had enough information on why Alfie was incarcerated for the moment. "What has he been saying?"

Alfie scanned the room; Annie wasn't sure what he was looking for because it was empty and the door was closed. The young man leant in conspiratorially and dropped the volume of his voice.

"He was talking about a bomb," Alfie said, whispering. "A home made one he'd been fixing together before he was locked up. He was joking around, laughing about what he'd put in the vest, that kind of thing. Only…"

Alfie broke off what he was saying to glance around the room again. Annie couldn't help but look over her shoulder, the feeling that someone was watching was all consuming, like they were breathing down her neck. Though when she turned there was no one there, just the silent flashing of the camera in the corner and the shadow of the guard through the reinforced glass in the door.

"Only what, Alfie?" Swift prompted.

"He was bigging himself up, like," Alfie went on. "Spouting about how he was going to get his own back and how he was gonna do it while he was still inside so no-one would suspect him."

"Do you know what kind of explosive he was talking about?" Annie asked. "Or who he wanted to get revenge on?"

"Dunno," Alfie shrugged and leant back in his chair, snapping the tension in the room.

Annie felt her chest expand and her shoulders drop with the movement. It was as though Alfie held court, bending and moulding the space around him with such force it affected the other people near him too. He was charismatic, that's for sure.

Swift uncrossed his arms, nodding. "Alfie," he said, slowly. "Can I ask why you wanted to talk to us about this? Why *us* specifically, why not just tell a guard or call the police about it?"

Picking at a piece of dry skin at the edge of his thumb nail, Alfie chewed on his bottom lip with a perfect row of white teeth. He took his time in answering, so much so that Annie wasn't sure he was going to answer at all. But when he met her eyes, she couldn't look away, hooked on what he was about to say.

"I know about your case," he said, simply. "And I wanted to help."

———

GETTING OUT OF THE PRISON TOOK THE SAME rigmarole as getting in. Annie and Swift stood silently as they were handed back their belongings and escorted back off the premises. Taking in great gulps of fresh air, Annie looked up at the grey sky and was glad to be out.

"How the hell does he know about the case?" she asked as they walked back to Swift's car. "Even the press doesn't know about the case, do they? Who's blabbed?"

Swift's head was dipped as he walked, eyes glued on his phone like a teenager who'd just been handed it back after a ban.

"Swift?" Annie pressed, circling in front of him to get his attention.

He didn't look up, treading on her foot and bumping her with his phone, startled. Annie felt her balance wobble with a lurch; she managed to right herself and held her ground, her heart thumping.

"Sorry, Annie." Swift looked up then, almost surprised to see her there.

Annie reached out a hand, placing it over his as he grasped his phone. "Everything okay, Swift?"

"Henry Chance is dead," he said, his eyebrows drawn together.

"Who?" Annie recognised the name but couldn't place it.

Swift looked up from his phone at Annie. They stood together for a beat, Annie's hand on Swift's, Swift's eyes on Annie. A cool breeze lifted Annie's hair and tickled the back of her neck, instead of enjoying the sensation of fresh air, it felt like an omen. They walked on.

"Henry Chance," Swift repeated. "The man Jessica was prosecuting. He was found dead this morning before they could recall him for the verdict."

"This feels like more than a coincidence," Annie said, glancing back over her shoulder at the prison looming overhead, a sky scape of dark swirling clouds behind it. "I don't like this, Swift. Not one little bit."

FOURTEEN

"WHERE ARE WE GOING?" ANNIE ASKED AS SWIFT HIT the gas pedal and sped around the ring road.

"Straight to the hospital to see Evans," Swift replied. "He's finalising the autopsy of Chance now and I want to go speak to him first."

Annie held onto the door as Swift spun around a roundabout and doubled back out onto the dual carriageway to the hospital. Annie had met Evans on numerous occasions now, as he was the local pathologist they normally crossed paths in the saddest of ways. He was calm and good at his job, giving the MCU the facts they needed to secure an arrest. More than once he'd made Annie's brain work in different ways. She liked the black and white of the autopsy results, they were scientific and honest, unlike most of the people she met on the cases.

"So how *did* Alfie know about the case?" Annie asked again as the car sped towards the hospital.

"It's out," Swift replied, not taking his eyes off the road. "God knows how but the press have gotten a hold of it and it's on their radar; some of them have it up on their websites today and I'm sure it'll hit the headlines in the morning."

"We need to find Jessica then," Annie said, scanning her phone for articles. "If there are images of her, she could be vulnerable to attack.

"People won't want to go near her, surely?" Swift said, pulling into a parking bay.

"You'd think, and mostly they will keep away," Annie agreed. "But you'll always get those who want to be a part of something like this. Likes and views and clicks and whatever. And having strangers around her at the moment is a bad idea. Can we bring her in and keep her safe?"

Swift killed the engine and they sat in silence as it ticked over.

"We can't though, can we?" he said, shifting in his seat to face Annie. "Because if we bring her in, how is she going to do the tasks that are being asked of her?"

Swift pulled out his phone again and swiped at the screen.

"Tink," he said, eyes on Annie. "I need you and Page to go bring Luke Hart in, we need to find out if he knows what's going on and if he's got anything to do with it. Annie and I are with Evans; Henry Chance is dead."

He said his goodbyes and pocketed his phone.

127

"Shall we?" he asked, and for the first time in a long time, Annie wanted to say no. She wanted to just sit with him in his car and pretend this wasn't going on around her. To while away the weekend doing normal things like hoovering and housework, watching Swift making pies and salads for lunch, or taking the non-existent dog for a walk. She searched his face for a hint that he'd like to be doing the same, but there was nothing but creeping concern. "Annie?"

"Let's go," she said, ignoring the pit of concern in her stomach.

EVANS WAS AT HIS DESK, A HALF EATEN DOUBLE Decker lay open next to the keyboard as he tapped away at the keys. Even in the office part of the lab, Annie could still smell the underlying stench of formaldehyde and raw meat and she swallowed heavily at the idea of eating in there. Keyboards were gross enough back in the station office she worked in, she couldn't imagine what this place would look like under a black light.

Evans turned and gave them a wide smile and Annie felt guilty for doubting his cleanliness. Evans was the epitome of professional, there's no way his keyboard was anyway near as bad as some of Annie's uniformed compadres.

"Joe, Annie," Evans rose from his chair like Goliath and shook their hands. "I'd like to say it's good to see you, but the circumstances never feel right. We need to meet out of work sometime so I can mean it when I say it."

"You're never not at work though, Evans," Swift joked.

"Too true," Evans replied. "Too true. You're here for Mr Chance, I assume?"

"Sadly, yep," Annie said.

Evans rolled his chair back under his desk and out of the way and led Annie and Swift through the plastic strip curtain to the mortuary. The steel gurney in the middle of the room was empty, the spotlight above it reflected in the shiny metal. Evans flicked a switch and the spotlight blossomed, flowering light around the spotless room. Heading to the mortuary fridge, Evans unlocked a door and rolled out a gurney, a black body bag taking up most of the trolley space.

Annie watched as Evans pulled the autopsy table over to the fridge and gently slid the body bag from one to the other, respectful in his movements, careful not to bump or snag the material. He closed the fridge and pushed the gurney back under the spotlight. Breathing through her mouth, Annie stepped forward as Evans unzipped the bag and revealed the body of Henry Chance.

Some dead people look like they're sleeping to Annie, not Henry Chance, there was nothing peaceful about his death mask. Evans pulled the bag open to show them his whole body, the autopsy stitches a Y shape across his chest and torso.

"Not much to see there, Annie," Evans said as Annie leant forward to look at the body. "No outward signs of any wrongdoing."

"How did he die?" Swift asked. "Who the hell got near enough to Chance to kill him?"

"Unsure about that one, Joe," Evans went on. "But there is something I can tell you."

He bent forwards and, with forceps, bent Chance's nose to the side. Annie saw the damage to the man's septum which had left it thin and red raw.

"Drug user," Swift said. "Do you think it was drugs that killed him?"

"Was he involved with drugs?" Evans asked.

"I honestly don't know enough about the case to answer that," Swift replied. "We need to go and check it out. Anything else you can tell us about Chance?"

Evans started zipping back up the bag, careful not to catch any of Chance's skin or hair as he went.

"I've sent samples to the lab for toxicology, I'll let you know when the reports come back," Evans said. "Looked like there might have been traces of white substance in Chance's nostrils too, and I'll forward on anything I find."

"Thanks, Evans," Annie said. "He would have been breaking his bail conditions if he was taking drugs while awaiting sentencing."

Evans nodded, his lips pursed. "That doesn't put off as many people as you'd think, sadly."

"Tell me about it," Annie replied, thinking back to

her probation days when drugs were a recall threat that was regularly ignored.

They thanked Evans and left him to put Chance's body back in the storage fridges with a promise to send over the tox report as soon as it was back.

"Do you think this is linked to our case?" Swift asked Annie as they walked back along the windowless corridor to the exit of the morgue.

Annie took her time to answer, the same thoughts had been going round and round in her head.

"I don't know," she answered, honestly. "It could be a coincidence that Jessica's client has been killed, Chance could have been the target of revenge for what he did to his girlfriend. There's no saying what any parent would do to protect their child, and when keeping them protected fails, revenge can sometimes feel like the only answer. But also…"

Annie stopped walking, turning instead to look at Swift. The corridor was empty, the hum of machinery and strip lights dotting the silence with a current that Annie could practically feel.

"Jessica was delayed in getting back to court," she went on. "Henry Chance would have been safely in court or, from all accounts, jail, if Jessica had been available for the jury's decision. What is the likelihood that Jessica and Henry aren't connected? Though the MOs are completely off whack with each other, a possible drugging, and a maniac with explosives and a crazy to do list. But isn't it too coincidental? And you told me that coincidences don't happen, that they're for lazy people."

Swift furrowed his brow, his lips lifting slightly. "I don't remember adding that bit."

Annie tilted her head to the side, drawing her lower lip in between her teeth and clasping it there. She wanted to say so many things to Swift, not just about the case, but a mortuary corridor was not the time nor the place. She could feel an elastic connection between them, tightening around her chest the longer they stood together in the empty, electric corridor.

"Where now?" she asked, throatily.

"I say we go and pay Pete a visit," Swift replied, taking Annie's arm and slotting it through his own. "I would kill for a pizza."

They stepped out of the corridor into the evening gloom.

"Well you're in the wrong place to do that, Swift," Annie joked. "Everyone here is already dead."

FIFTEEN

"HOW ARE THINGS, O'MALLEY?" SWIFT WASHED THE last of his BBQ chicken pizza down with a slosh of red wine and wiped his face with the polka dot paper napkin.

Annie quickly took a bite of her veggie supreme so she didn't have to answer straight away. Pete's Pizza was heaving, they'd been lucky to get a table at all, even though it was late on a Sunday when they'd turned up. Pete had squeezed his favourite upstairs neighbour into a booth right at the back near the kitchen door and Annie could hear him whistling away as he prepped his pizzas with gusto. The smells of dough and melted cheese mingled with garlic oil and pepperoni. Pete had been an ear for Annie to talk to and a shoulder to cry on more than once in the last ten years she'd lived in the flat above his pizzeria, and she was buzzed his business was doing so well.

Taking a glug of Malbec, Annie turned her attention from Pete's dough throwing to Swift, who was looking at her across the table with tired eyes. A candle flickered in between them, but the bright light from the kitchen drowned out its touch. Swift had taken off his jacket and undone his shirt collar, rolling his sleeves up to his elbows.

"Work things?" she replied, eventually. "Or life things?"

The patter of noise from the busy restaurant meant they could happily talk shop without being overheard if that's what Swift had meant.

"Every things," he said, picking up the menu and looking through the list of desserts. "Work, family, life... love?"

Annie felt her wine go down the wrong way and coughed loudly to clear her airways, her nose stinging. Swift was still engrossed in the desserts, seemingly not realising the impact of his words.

"Um... well," Annie started. "Mim and I were supposed to be off for a spa day yesterday, but obviously that has been postponed."

Across the table, Swift peered over his menu. "A spa day with your estranged sister? I hope you weren't heading to Paradise Grove?"

He chuckled. Paradise Grove had been their last case together, a luxury spa hotel with added death and destruction. Annie and Swift had stayed together in a twin room but hadn't been able to enjoy the facilities, so Annie thought she'd treat herself and her sister to something similar when the case had closed.

"Is that place still open?" Annie asked, taking the menu from Swift even though she knew she was having a Strawberry Sundae for pudding.

"I think it's probably floating out in the North Sea by now," Swift shook his head. "It was practically dipping its toes when we stayed there. Will you rebook?"

Annie shrugged, sipping her wine. "The idea was to spend time together that wasn't quite so full on. A spa made sense because it's so relaxing, but maybe I just need to get it over with and invite her over for dinner one day. We need to talk about our parents."

"That's for sure," Swift agreed.

Annie's dad had abducted Mim as a toddler when Annie was just a teenager. Annie's relationship with her mum had been loving but difficult and, up until a few months ago, she was the only family Annie had. Mim had been adamant she'd not been abducted, but rather rescued from a mum who was dangerous and had killed a man. Annie hadn't wanted to hear any more about their history since Mim had told her, but her interest was piqued now time had passed and the anger had simmered.

"What do you think I should do?" Annie asked Swift, as Pete sauntered over to the table, a tea towel slung over his shoulder.

"Can I get you two sweeties some desserts?" Pete winked at Annie, a nudge to the friendship that had developed between her and Swift that Pete was hoping would blossom into something more.

"Usual, please," Annie replied, smiling. "With extra whipped cream and cherries today."

Pete smacked his lips. "And for you, sir?"

"I'll have the same," Swift said to Pete, his eyes not leaving Annie's. "She's got good taste."

Pete whisked the menu from Annie and sauntered back into the kitchen as his staff brought him more orders and took out the plates that were ready.

"What do I think you should do?" Swift asked, going back to their conversation. "You can't cook her dinner at your flat, you've only got a kitchenette and that's barely functioning. Why don't you invite her to mine, you can have free rein of the place. I can go out if you want me to, or hide upstairs. That way you've got time and space to talk in a place you feel comfortable in. At least, I hope you feel comfortable there?"

Swift lived in a turreted Victorian mansion on the outskirts of the city and Annie felt more at home there than she did at her Mum's place.

"Thank you, Joe," Annie said. "That's kind of you. I might take you up on that when this case is over."

Swift leant forward across the table, his forearms leaning on the Formica.

"It's no spa, but I can give you a massage if you like." His eyes twinkled with the candlelight below his chin.

"How do you feel about feet?" Annie said, laughing. "I was going to have a pedicure."

Swift recoiled dramatically. "Nope. Not feet.

Nope. Not even your feet, O'Malley, sorry. I draw a line there."

"Not even *my* feet?" Annie lifted a brow, teasingly.

Swift's eyes darkened, his lids dropped heavily but his gaze didn't falter from Annie's. A silence fell over the table, punctuated by Swift tapping a finger on the stem of his wine glass.

"What do you think about the case?" he asked, clearing his throat, and pulling his shoulders back. "Where are we at?"

Annie felt the tug of tension between them twang free and sat back in her chair.

"I had a look at the tracker and Jessica hasn't moved from her apartment since we left with Sunday the cat." Annie grimaced. "Which was yesterday if I remember correctly. Days often feel a bit hazy during cases, don't they?"

Swift laughed, kindly. "Mine are like that most of the time, I blame my age!"

"You're the same age as me, near enough, way too young to be blaming that for anything."

"Debatable." Swift rubbed his hands in glee as Pete placed their puddings on the table. "Thanks Pete."

"If Jessica hasn't left her apartment, and we've not heard from her," Annie spoke, dipping her spoon through the cream to the ice-cream below. "Chances are she's not been given her next test yet."

"I can't think it'll be long though," Swift agreed.

"Since she was taken on Friday, she's had…" he counted them out on his fingers as he spoke. "Shakespeare graffiti on Friday evening. Straight into the poisoning on Saturday early hours. The cat smuggling was Saturday afternoon, and then orders to kill said cat on Saturday night."

"Your face is saying a thousand words." Annie licked her spoon. "Are you thinking it's been a long time, too?"

"They were all bunched together, frantic and pressured over the last two days," Swift nodded. "We haven't heard a thing all day."

"I suppose even arch nemeses and crazy madmen still need their day of rest." Annie almost chuckled. "But we should check up on her."

"I'll get uniform to do it," Swift replied. "They're watching the doors anyway."

He pulled out his phone and Annie took the opportunity to dig into her sundae as Swift spoke to dispatch and asked them to check up on Jessica.

"How many more tasks do you think there'll be?" Annie asked, feeling the sundae stick in her throat. "Jessica can't go on indefinitely, can she?"

She knew what that meant. When all the tasks were over there would be no need for the pawn anymore.

"They've escalated quite quickly." Swift popped a cherry in his mouth and chewed around the stone. "We've gone from some quite harmless graffiti to the killing of an innocent cat."

"Thankfully not actually, though," Annie said. "And I'm not sure how innocent Sunday will be feeling when I get home. How wrecked do you think my place will be?"

"It'll be fine." Swift drew out the words, his pitch high.

"He wrecked a thirty grand painting, Joe!"

"Then be thankful that everything you own is tucked away in that filing cabinet that masquerades as your wardrobe."

Annie reached over the table and hit Swift gently on the shoulder. "Oy." She stole a cherry from his sundae as punishment and popped it in her mouth. "Just because you've got a sprawling home and more storage than I could shake a cat at, doesn't mean you use it. I've seen your clothes strewn all over your bedroom floor."

Pete arrived at that moment to check up on their desserts.

"Ooh," he sang. "I bet you have."

He gave a little bow and backed away.

"What's the plan for tomorrow?" Annie asked, ignoring the blush rising on Swift's face.

The cafe had quietened as they'd been eating their desserts, and a lull fell over the space.

"Hopefully we'll have some tox results back on Chance," Swift said, concentrating on getting the last of his ice cream from the glass. "And I think we need to talk to the work colleague and the ex, see what they have to say about things. Are you okay to be in the office first thing?"

"Of course," Annie said, wiping her mouth with her napkin and finishing her wine. "I think I'll find it hard to sleep anyway, knowing what Jessica is going through."

"I think I'm going to find it hard to sleep at all," Swift replied, putting his spoon between his lips and cleaning off the last of the sundae. "Not until this is over. One way or another, we need to get that vest away from Jessica and away from everyone else. But there's no way of knowing how it's attached or if that will trigger it."

"Imagine how claustrophobic that must be starting to feel," Annie said, puffing out her cheeks. "If it was me, I'd have tried to get rid of the vest almost immediately."

The thought of being trapped in something so close to her skin, made Annie shudder and she wondered just how long Jessica had left before she did something rash.

SIXTEEN

MONDAY

LUKE HART WAS LIKE A SPRINGER SPANIEL PUPPY DOG in a standard issue tracksuit. Annie was getting antsy sitting across the interview table from him and from the twitch in Swift's temple he was too.

"Luke," Annie began, anything to stop him rambling nonsensically about missing breakfast and getting out of laundry duty. "You're well known for your electronics. Can you tell us if you've built anything recently that you shouldn't have?"

Annie was playing to his ego. His case file had been peppered with incidents that had been triggered by Luke Hart trying to show off his explosive skills inside. With each failed squib, Luke's sentence increased, and it looked like it was on an exponential rise.

"I can't help it if my au naturel skills keep on keeping on, can I?" Luke sat back in his chair, legs outstretched, shackled hands behind his head.

Annie bit her tongue, determined not to pull him up on his error. Though perhaps calling his skills simple was a Freudian Slip and not just the idiocy of a man trying to sound clever.

"Tell us more?" Annie asked, widening her eyes, pouting a little, and hating herself for it.

She saw Swift take a glance at her before turning his attention back to the young man with greasy hair and roving eyes.

"I blew up the showers in the C block," Luke said, grinning like the Cheshire Cat. "Boom."

Annie had read about this particular incident in the files that morning. Luke Hart had mixed cleaner with bicarb and thrown it down the drains in the communal showers. It was less of a *boom* and more of a clever way to unblock the sweat and grease balls that lodged just under the tiles.

"I bet the others loved that," Annie went on. They'd made a pact to let her do all the talking during this interview, Annie felt Luke would respond better to a female than an attractive male, and she wasn't wrong.

"Yeah, they were well chuffed." Luke chewed on his tongue as though it was gum.

"Anything else," Annie prompted. "Anything outside of prison that you're involved in?"

The man's jaw stopped; he dropped his hands down onto the table with a clatter.

"Like what?" He was wary now. "Them guards who brought me here were talking about a bomb. But how could I have anything to do with a real bomb when I've been stuck inside for twenty-four months?"

"There are ways of communicating with the outside world though, aren't there?" Annie pressed. "And a smart guy like you would have all the knows."

Luke puffed out his chest, but there was no beating on it this time. He looked like the wind had been taken from his sails.

"I ain't got no mobile phone," he said, glancing at the door to the interrogation room. "Some of them in there have tiny ones, like prehistoric phones that they can't even get online with. But not me. I... er... I don't need one. Got no one to contact, have I?"

His eyes dropped to the table.

"What about people you hung around with before you were sentenced?" Annie probed, feeling a little sorry for him until she remembered he'd blown up cats. "Friends with the same *tastes* as you?"

Annie could feel her guard slipping, the more she thought about Sunday and how he'd poked his little orange nose in her face that morning. As she'd left for work, he'd meowed happily and curled up on the paperwork on her desk. How anyone could hurt Sunday, or any other innocent animal was beyond her. And Luke was coming across as a guy who liked to big himself up but had no real brains behind why or how to do it.

"Weren't no one," Luke's voice wavered at Annie's change in tone. "What's going on? I thought I was here to talk about my bombs and how much trouble I was in. A ticking off. Do you want to know about the time I set fire to the kitchen and nearly blew the cooker door off its hinges?"

Annie had read about that too, a simple case of leaving the gas on for longer than needed before hitting the pilot light. She shrugged, her mouth narrowing.

"Who do you blame for being in prison, Luke?" Swift piped up, catching Annie's reticence.

Luke shrugged. "My own stupid fault for getting caught, weren't it? Look, I don't mean to be rude but why is yous going on about outside? I'm in for a long stretch and I'm making the most of it. There's no reason for me to be talking about the outside. I'm cosy where I am."

"Why were you talking about getting revenge?" Annie asked, her voice back. "About being in contact with someone to *reap what they sowed*, or something along those lines?"

Luke looked put out, his face folded into creases.

"I ain't been talking to no-one, I ain't no grass."

Annie shook her head. "Thanks for your time, Mr Hart."

Swift spoke into the tape and ended the interview

as Annie pushed her chair back from the table and opened the door. As the prison officers walked Luke back through the rear corridors to their van outside, Annie marched to the incident room and studied the boards.

"I trust your judgement, O'Malley," Swift said, closing the door behind him. "But would you care to let me in on your thoughts? How can you be so sure that Mr *Boom* isn't our man?"

Swift make a noise like a small explosion, his hands mimicking a blast. Annie laughed, glad of the distraction. She perched on the table, propping her feet up on a chair. Behind her the photos of Jessica, Luke, and Henry were still pinned to the board with more questions than answers.

"He's not clever enough to do this," Annie said, shaking her head. "Luke Hart is all talk. Those explosions he was on about were little more than damp squibs. He may very well think he's all that when it comes to explosives, and perhaps on the outside he was able to put together a layman's device, but this is far too complex for his skills. And he certainly doesn't have the wherewithal to fashion a macabre game of dare."

"But what about what Alfie overheard?" Swift asked, sitting down on a chair next to Annie's feet.

"The cellmate?" Annie asked, and Swift nodded. "He was chancing his luck, maybe? Knew what was going on out here and knew what Luke was in for. He may very well have overheard Luke talking about revenge and what not, but Luke is not our guy."

"Which takes us right back to square one." Swift puffed out his cheeks and looked beyond Annie to the notice board. "Where to now?"

"Have we managed to get hold of Jessica at home?" Annie asked.

But before Swift could reply the door opened and Page stuck his head in the room. "Guys, there's someone in reception I think you're going to want to talk to."

———

ANNIE RECOGNISED THE MAN FROM JESSICA'S apartment. He seemingly recognised Annie too.

"You!" Dylan Burrows pointed a finger in her direction as she approached Jessica's colleague.

"Mr Burrows." Annie stopped short at adding the multitude of letters after his name. "My name is Annie O'Malley, this is DI Swift. How can we help you today?"

Dylan Burrows had the sunken, red eyed look of a man who'd spent his weekend snorting a large proportion of his wages up his nose. Annie wondered if that's why he seemed so cocky when he'd arrived at Jessica's apartment on Saturday.

"It's Jessica," he said through clenched teeth. "I'm worried about her."

"What are your concerns?" Swift asked.

"She hasn't turned up for work yet," Dylan went on, his arms crossed over his chest, his foot tapping on the lino in the quiet reception. "I came in to file a missing person's report."

"We're appreciative of your concern, Mr Burrows," Swift said. "But we are aware of Jessica's presence at her apartment, she's just helping us with our enquiries at the moment and is unable to come to work."

"So that's why she couldn't make court?" Dylan's face was knotted with questions. "That's why Henry Chance was killed? Because she was helping you with some enquiries?"

Swift stood up to his full height, pulling his shoulders back.

"The death of Henry Chance is not down to any error of the police force, or Jessica Frampton." Swift's face said a thousand more words.

"Yeah, but I bet you haven't caught who did it, yet?" Dylan cocked his chin towards Swift.

"That's not our department, Mr Burrows," Annie replied.

"But it would seem that looking after people who are under your care isn't your department either." Dylan looked at Annie now, his eyes narrow.

"What do you mean by that, Mr Burrows." Annie held in her frustrations; she was fed up of alpha males trying to exert their presumed dominance through silly little word games.

Dylan cocked his head, as though wondering

whether to tell her. Annie felt like punching him in the balls to see if that would work, but she didn't think that would go down well.

"I went to Jessica's apartment," Dylan said, eventually, a wash of worry on his face when he finally looked properly at Annie. "This morning. I was worried about her, especially after not being let in to see her on Saturday. We've got some work stuff to sort out. The door was open, so I went in. The place is empty. Jessica isn't there. Just find her, will you. I need to know where she is."

Annie felt her stomach drop out from underneath her. She grabbed her phone from her pocket and swiped to the *find a friend* app. There was Jessica's dot, quite clearly over the space on the map where her apartment building was situated. Only, if Dylan Burrows was right, Jessica had stolen out from under the noses of the uniforms tasked to keep watch, ditched the tag and with it she'd ditched her only chance to stay safe.

SEVENTEEN

"How did she slip past the police protection?" Annie shouted out to Swift as they raced towards the car park.

"A hood and a pair of dark glasses might do it with that lot," Swift replied, beeping open his 4x4 and jumping into the driver's seat.

Tink and Page were on their way to the apartment to try and track down Erinn and find out what had happened there. The officers who'd entered the flat on Swift's word said it looked as though the place had been ransacked, but when they divulged what that had been based on, both Swift and Annie realised it was the work of Sunday the cat and not an intruder.

"Right," Swift said, pressing the ignition and turning to Annie. "Where to?"

Annie was about to ask *why me* when she realised that was her role in the team, second guessing people, working out what they were thinking sometimes before even they did. She took a moment, staring out the windscreen at the drizzle collecting patiently each time it was cleared away by the wipers. She assumed Jessica knew about the death of the man she had been prosecuting, perhaps she'd gone to see her client. Maybe she'd heard that Luke Hart had been talking, could she have tried to make a visitation to see him.

Annie looked down at her fingers, feeling like a fraud as she picked away at the skin on her thumbnails. A petal of blood blossomed across her cuticle, and she put her thumb to her mouth, sucking it clean.

"My mum always told me that sucking my thumb would make my teeth stick out," Swift said, holding her gaze for a beat.

"That's it, what an idiot," Annie cried, wiping her thumb clean on her trousers instead.

"Well, I stopped," Swift replied, indignant. "Look, my teeth are pretty straight."

He gave Annie a beaming smile, not that she needed him to. Annie knew Swift had perfectly straight, white teeth, with a tiny little gap between the front two that she thought was cute.

"Not you." She smiled back. "Me…"

"You obviously didn't suck your thumb when you were younger, either." He looked confused.

"Not my teeth, Swift," Annie said, buckling up. "My mind. It took me a little longer than I hoped to get here, I guess I'm a bit distracted at the moment, but Jessica's a mum, and wherever her boy is I bet that's where we'll find her."

"As unidiotic as they come, O'Malley," Swift said, searching his notepad and punching the address into his SatNav. "Anthony Marble, here we come."

***

JESSICA HAD OBVIOUSLY BEEN THE MAIN EARNER IN their relationship. Marble's house was a terrace, ex-council by the looks of the grey, concrete facade. He lived in a less than desirable area in the city, but Annie noticed the cut grass and the bulbs poking their heads through the soil.

"Can I help you?" The man who answered the door was tall and thin, and the mop of blond hair on his head made Annie's mind head directly to the reeds that grew up between sand dunes.

"DI Swift and Annie O'Malley," Swift said, flashing his badge. "Can we come in?"

"Is this about Jessica?" Marble opened the door wide and ushered the officers inside.

A young boy came running down the hallway towards them, skidding to a stop on the polished floorboards.

"Daddy, look at me, look at me," he shouted, laughing, before spinning around and around in one spot and staggering back away.

"Oliver, love," Marble bent down and caught the young boy, lifting him high and blowing raspberries on his belly which made him squeal with happiness. "Daddy's got to talk to these two people, why don't you go and put on cartoons, and I'll come get you when I'm done?"

Oliver didn't need telling twice, he scrambled from his dad's arms and ran off down the corridor waving his arms in the air, screaming something about Peppa Pig. Annie laughed, kindly.

"He's lovely," she said, following Marble as he led them past the living room where Oliver was sitting a few inches away from a giant screen, and down to the kitchen at the back of the house.

The kitchen had been knocked through to the lean-to and the space was open and bright, even though the paint was dark green. Plants took up most of the free space and gave the room the feel of an orangery.

"He's a whirlwind, but yes, he's lovely." Marble pulled out a stool from the small island and ushered Annie and Swift to sit on the squashy sofa.

"Can I ask why you mentioned Jessica?" Annie asked, feeling the sofa sag to the middle as Swift sat down. She righted herself so she didn't end up in his lap.

"It's just that she was supposed to collect Oliver last night," Marble said, fiddling with a coaster, twisting it around in his fingers. "And she's not picking up her phone. I had to take emergency leave from work. It's very unusual for Jessica to be late at all, let alone a whole night late."

"Have you had any contact at all from her?" Swift asked.

Marble shook his head. "Sometimes she'll call to say goodnight to Oliver, but that's not usual. We like it to be a clean cut with each parent, you know? Unless Oliver wants to talk to either of us, which he knows he can do at any time he likes. I know she's working a case at the moment, so I wondered if that had gotten complicated." He looked down at the wooden worktop, chewing his top lip. "But I have never known Jess not to let me know if the plans change. Is she okay?"

Annie thought back to how Erinn had described Anthony Marble as a *useless twat* and so far, she wasn't seeing that at all. She knew there were always two sides to a story, her own life had taught her that well, so Erinn was probably standing up for Jessica after the breakup.

"We spoke to Jessica on Saturday, and I can tell you that she was okay then," Annie said, diplomatically, not sure how much to divulge. "But can you think of anyone who'd want to hurt Jessica? Any past cases who've sent letters from prison? Any family members who've been threatening after she's successfully prosecuted their bother or son?"

Marble laughed ironically. "Only all of the cases she ever worked on," he said. "She's the best at her job. And she always tells me of backlash she's getting just in case it affects Oliver when he's with me."

"Was there anything recently?" Swift asked.

"Nothing out of the ordinary." Marble pursed his lips and tapped at them with his fingers. "There had been the usual DVs, she gets a lot of those, but their families don't tend to get too vocal about it, too embarrassed I'd think. Drugs are always abundant around here, it's a city in the middle of nowhere with not a great nightlife, rife for County Lines."

"Did Jessica ever prosecute the kids caught up in County Lines?" Annie asked, referring to the mules that were hired by gangs to transport their wares. Mostly underage, always vulnerable.

Marble shook his head. "Not really," he said. "She was more interested in higher up the food chain. There have been a few, she's jailed a couple of midway men. Not the creme de la creme, more the ones who think they're something, who get to boss around the kids who sell. There's always beef between the gangs around here. You wouldn't think it to look at it, but there are some dangerous boundaries that you wouldn't want to cross."

"Boundaries?" Annie asked.

"Yeah, you know, the areas the gangs sell in, that kind of thing." He put down the coaster and crossed his arms over his chest. "And there has been some strong stuff out there in the last few weeks, too. I've seen more than my share of drug related death recently."

"What is it you do, Mr Marble?" Swift asked.

"I'm an A&E nurse, for my sins. The jobs erratic, the hours are cruel, but I love it," he laughed again, pushing himself up from the stool. "I'm sorry, I didn't offer you a drink. Can I get either of you a tea or coffee?"

"No thank you, Mr Marble," Swift said, rising from the sofa. "We'd best be on our way. Thank you for your time, please can you let us know as soon as you hear from Jessica?"

Annie toppled into the space left by Swift, and he offered her a hand up.

"So you don't know where she is right now?" Marble asked, wide eyed. "Why are you asking me if I know of anyone who could do her harm?"

"We're working on a case with Jessica at the moment and can't divulge that," Swift replied, hoiking Annie to her feet.

"Will you ask her to get in touch with me, too," Marble went on, his shoulders stooped. "If you hear from her first."

"Of course we will," Annie said, disappointment sitting heavily in her rib cage that Jessica wasn't with Oliver.

She popped her head into the living room on her way out to say goodbye to the young boy, but he'd moved from the television.

"Oliver?" Annie said, stepping fully into the room.

The little boy was nowhere to be seen. Annie was about to call Anthony from the hallway where he was saying goodbye to Swift, when she saw the curtains twitch. Creeping up to the window, Annie pulled gently at the corner of the heavy material, expecting Oliver to jump out in a game of hide and seek. But he didn't move, he was too busy waving at a figure across the street, peeking out from behind the safety of a tree. A figure Annie recognised. Jessica Frampton.

EIGHTEEN

"JESSICA?" ANNIE SHOUTED AS SHE RAN OUT OF THE door and into the empty street. "Jessica wait."

Swift followed hot on her heels, Anthony Marble left standing in the doorway with confusion on his face.

Scanning the street, Annie couldn't see where Jessica had fled. To her right was a dead end for cars but a small pathway led towards an alley. To her left was the main road. The morning air was thick with fog, the ground underfoot crunched with ice. Jessica had been wearing her thin coat and Annie couldn't bear to think about how cold she must be.

"What did you see?" Swift asked from a few paces behind her.

Annie swung to face him.

"It was Jessica," she said, her chest rising and falling with the exertion. "She was at the window talking to Oliver. But she ran off when she saw me."

"Which way?"

"I didn't see," Annie replied, her head swinging back and forth with the options. "But my guess is that way."

She pointed towards the alleyway and broke into a run, hoping her intuition would once again prove her right.

"Jessica," she shouted as the walls of the alley loomed over her. "Please let us help you."

Broken glass crunched underfoot; the stench of urine filled Annie's nose. Discarded carrier bags and fast food boxes littered the space, and Annie slowed, treading carefully.

"What do you think has happened?" Swift asked, jogging beside her.

"She wanted to see Oliver," Annie panted. "But why is she running from us?"

"Maybe she's scared we'll keep her away from him," Swift replied. "Watch out, Annie, let me go first."

Up ahead the alleyway bent to the right. There was no way of seeing what was past the brick walls that trapped them in its arteries and the stench of urine was fast being replaced by the thick cloying smell of weed. Annie slowed to a walk, letting Swift pass in front of her, his hand on her shoulder. Annie knew she could probably take on whatever was there, no doubt a group of teens enjoying an early morning smoke between school lessons, but she appreciated the thought none the less.

She was right; a small group of four boys who looked no older than fifteen huddled around the bright tip of the biggest joint Annie had ever seen. Dirty tracksuits hung off their thin frames, their hair a carbon copy of each other's close cut clip.

"What's going on here?" Swift asked, loudly.

"Never you mind, old man," one of the boys spat back at him. "Buggar off back to your residential home."

The group laughed, passing the joint between themselves as though it was a bag of popcorn.

"I'll mind so long as I see something illegal going on." Swift drew out his badge and flashed it at the kids.

Their demeanour changed faster than their allegiances to the guy who'd spoken.

"Crap, man," the tallest of the group yelled. "We're just trying to enjoy ourselves."

Swift walked up to them, slowly, surely, and took the joint right from between the lips of a boy whose eyes were so wide he looked like a cartoon character. Throwing it to the floor, Swift crushed it with the heel of his shoe.

"What's say we pretend I never saw this," Swift went on. "If you can tell me which way the young woman went."

"What woman?" He jutted his chin towards Swift in an act of defiance that masked a death wish.

"Don't play silly beggars or I'll drag you all up to the station and charge you with obstructing the course of justice with a hefty dose of supplying illegal substances."

The young man did a jiggle, trying to make up his mind whether to square up to the DI or back down. Eventually common sense prevailed, and he stepped away, back to the safety of his gang of friends.

"That way," he pointed towards the exit of the alleyway.

"We know she was running this way," Swift said, exasperated. "Where did she go after that?"

"She turned towards the city." The shortest of the group, and by the look of his face, the youngest, spoke so quietly Annie barely heard what he said. "Please don't take us in. I'll get in so much trouble."

Annie felt the cogs turning in her mind, something Swift had said had triggered them and she was waiting for them to click into place.

"We're not going to take you in," she said, looking pointedly at Swift. "But you all need to get to school. You're ruining your futures standing here in the cold smoking what smells like a very strong joint. Why not at least stay warm and dry in class? I've worked with men like you who made the decision to stay out in the cold and let's just say, it's not often ended well."

The smallest of the four looked down at the ground and scuffed his worn trainers into the dirt. But the others looked less amused with her.

"It's just weed," one of them said, his knock off Adidas tracksuit too short in the arms and legs. "At least we're not snorting the hard stuff. Or injecting it. What's wrong with a smoke?"

Annie felt the pieces of the puzzle slot into place.

"There's nothing wrong with it," she went on, wondering how to broach what she needed to. "As long as you're old enough, at home, and not supposed to be in class. Doing it out here in an alleyway is asking for trouble."

"Maybe we like trouble," the taller one piped up, a sickening grin on his face.

"Then maybe we give you some trouble." Annie wasn't backing down.

"Poe, give over." The smallest grabbed the arm of the tallest and pulled him away from Annie.

Poe, that was ironic, given how unpoetic the boy was.

"Tell us one more thing," Annie continued, not intimidated at all by his presence. "And then we'll watch you leave, and I don't want to see any of you around here between classes again, deal?"

"Depends what you wanna know," Poe said, jaw set.

"You said it was just weed." Annie was undeterred. "But if I was trying to get hold of something stronger, where would I go? Who would I ask?"

"How the hell would I know," Poe shouted, kicking at the ground in front of him, eyeing up the end of the alleyway. "We only smoke weed. We don't do nothing stronger. Come on, lads, let's get out of here before we're shanked for being squealers."

Poe flipped Annie the bird as he slunk away, the other three following quickly behind him.

"You sounded just like my high school head mistress then," Swift chuckled as they watched the boys leave the alleyway.

Annie laughed. "Sorry, bring back bad memories for you?"

Swift contemplated that for a moment, looking at Annie as though trying to figure something out.

"Nope," he said, shaking his head. "Quite liked it actually."

He winked at Annie and turned to the exit of the alleyway, to where the boys had just disappeared.

"Urgh, Swift," Annie joked. "Did you just wink at me? I'm afraid I might have to disown you now."

"I only did it because I know how much you love it," Swift replied, winking again in an exaggerated manner.

Annie exited the alleyway, her head shaking, a smile on her lips. In the distance she saw the group of boys headed over the road and in the general direction of the school. A puff of smoke covered their heads like the cartoon of Pig-Pen from Charlie Brown. She saw them stop where a circle of trees with a bench around their circumference tried to give the area a bit of greenery. Willing with all her might that they didn't sit, the boys circled something out of sight before grabbing each other and running away as fast as they could. Annie felt the hairs on the back of her neck rise and clutched at Swift's jacket sleeve.

"With me," she said, breaking into a run.

The body of Jessica Frampton must have scared the boys away. She was slumped on the bench, around the back of the seating area, away from the path. Her hair draped over her face, obscuring it from view. But by the greyness of her hands and the way her head was propped up by the wooden seat, Jessica looked like she'd sat down and taken her last breath.

"Jessica." Annie ran towards her, calling her name.

No, no, please don't let me be too late.

Annie dropped to her knees, ignoring the pain from the gravel through her trouser as she did so. Carefully taking Jessica by the shoulders, Annie propped her upright and felt in her throat for a pulse. Moving her fingers around, Annie fell back onto her haunches with relief. There was a pulse, a strong pulse.

"Jessica," Annie said again, shaking her gently, peeling one eye open.

Jessica spluttered, pushing Annie away with such force that she fell onto her backside.

"Annie?" Jessica's eyes widened. "Oh god, Annie, I'm so sorry."

Swift knelt down beside Jessica, offering Annie a hand up. Taking it gratefully, Annie pulled herself up and sat next to Jessica on the bench. The woman was shaking, her hands grey with cold.

"Swift," Annie said quietly. "We need medical assistance here, asap."

Swift nodded and pulled out his phone, dialling the control room and making the request.

"Jessica," Annie turned her attention back to the young woman. "What happened? Why are you here?"

"I couldn't sleep at home," Jessica said. "I couldn't stay where Erinn was, put her in that much danger."

Jessica wouldn't meet Annie's eyes. She tugged at the sleeve of her jacket, biting at her lips which were already red raw.

"Why did you go and see Oliver?" Annie asked, a chill creeping down her neck, making the hairs on her head stand on end. "What's going on, Jessica?"

Jessica's eyes brimmed with tears, she blinked, and they ran down her cheeks. But her face showed no emotion other than the shivers of cold.

"Jessica?" Swift was back at her knees, his hands gently clasped around Jessica's.

"Look," the woman said, nodding to the phone on the bench beside her.

Annie lifted it as though it was the explosive and not the vest wrapped around Jessica. She pressed a button to bring it to life, clicking through the options as best she could, Annie found the messages and her heart sank to the floor.

Holding it out to Swift, Annie read what had been written.

Time to stop playing, JF. It's kill or be killed.

"What?" she gasped.

"Who?" Swift asked.

"I don't know yet," Jessica shrugged. "I don't know why or who. I'm waiting to be told. But I can't kill someone, I know that even if I don't know anything else. I can't kill someone."

And at the moment, as the world was shrinking around Annie and the two people beside her, the phone gave a loud shrill in her hands.

NINETEEN

WITH SHAKING HANDS, ANNIE CLICKED ON THE message. Scrolling across the screen, painfully aware of the time it was taking to read, flashbacks of having to digest messages one line at a time on a screen so small she felt like she needed to borrow someone's reading glasses.

"It's a weblink," Annie said, clicking backwards and forwards across the message. "I don't want to click on it with this phone in case it triggers something, Swift, get yours out and type this in the search."

She read out a series of numbers and letters, her voice breaking. Jessica sat as still as a stone, hands clasped in her lap, waiting.

"It's a video," Swift said, pushing up off his knees and sitting next to Annie on the bench. "Looks like it's real time too."

He tilted the phone for Annie to see. It looked like CCTV, the grainy black and white form of a young man leaning against a wall, waiting. Past the man, Annie could just about make out a row of shops, their signage too blurred to read. A digital timer in the bottom left corner gave today's date and by the hours, minutes, and seconds ticking by, it was a live stream.

"Where is that?" Annie asked, her hand over Swift's moving the phone so she could get a better look.

"*Who* is that?" Swift leant over Annie, holding the phone so Jessica could see. "Any ideas?"

Jessica shook her head, her eyes barely registering the video. "I can't kill someone." She muttered it over and over like a mantra.

"Swift," Annie whispered, manoeuvring herself to protect Jessica from their words as much as possible. "Can we send this to the tech guys? Get them to bring him in on the pretence of something else?"

"I don't know," Swift said, quietly. "Whoever is doing this, Annie, they must be watching this video right now. There's no way of bringing him in without alerting him that we know what's going on."

"Then what do we do?" Annie stared at Swift, wide eyed.

She knew people, she could deal with people, that's why they'd brought her into the team in the first place. But this kind of danger was way beyond her levels of comfort. One wrong move and people could get hurt. She glanced at Jessica, imagining what would happen if the explosive was detonated now. She'd be gone, Swift would be gone. There were cars and bikes trailing up and down the main road behind them, not one hundred feet away. They'd, more than likely, be gone too. Annie couldn't risk being at fault for so many people dying. The idea made bile rise in her throat, stinging her oesophagus with its tangy ripeness.

"Jessica, can you listen to me very carefully?" Swift was on his feet now. "What I'm going to ask of you may seem unfair, but I need you to know that we are working all hours behind the scenes to try and cancel the charges on the vest and keep you safe."

Annie looked between Jessica and Swift, neither of whom had an ounce of blood in their cheeks.

"What is it?" Jessica stuttered.

"I think we've found the end point for whoever it is doing this to you," he went on, pointing his phone in their direction again, the man on the video stream still waiting patiently on the street corner. "This man, whoever he is, has a severe threat to his life. We need to bring him into the station and try and work out what connection he has to you, if any. And if he can help us get to whoever has done this to you."

"There's no connection," Jessica looked on the verge of tears, her vulnerability incongruent with the lifestyle she was so used to. "I'd know if there was. I don't recognise that man."

She threw her arms out in frustration.

"What I need you to do," Swift went on. "Is take yourself to the middle of the nearest field and wait."

Annie's eyebrows shot up to her hair. Jessica dropped her head, her chin tucked into her chest.

"Minimise collateral damage." It wasn't a question; Jessica knew what Swift was asking her.

"Swift?" Annie said, pointedly. "What are you doing?"

Swift took Annie's arm and led her away from Jessica. "We have a duty of care, O'Malley."

"What about our duty of care to Jessica?" Annie gasped.

"We're doing what we can to keep her safe," Swift sighed.

"Are we?" Annie hissed. "Are we really? Could we not have taken her in to keep her safe? Could we not have tried to remove the vest? What are we *actually* doing to keep her safe, Swift? You tell me."

She could feel the blood pumping around her body, feel the pulse in her cheeks, the tightening of her throat.

"Annie, listen to me," Swift took her arms gently in his and stepped closer. "We need to make sure that no one gets hurt, Jessica included. I'm going to get a team of uniform to bring in the target, but we don't know what will happen if we do that, so I need to protect the public." He stole a look at Jessica then turned back to Annie, lowering his voice. "Look, honestly, are we any further on finding out who is doing this?"

Annie shook her head, knowing but not wanting to admit that they had no idea who was behind the explosive. Before she'd met him, Annie had been almost certain it was Luke Hart, but now he was off the cards, they were back to square one. Jessica had a list ten miles long of people she'd successfully prosecuted, there was no way of whittling it down by talking to them all before her time was over.

"Then this man, whoever he is, could be our clue to finding him," Swift added, his thumbs rubbing comfortingly over Annie's sleeves.

But it wasn't Annie who needed comforting, it was Jessica.

"I'll go and make sure she's okay," Annie said, her heart sinking. "Bring him in if you need to but give Jessica some time to get to somewhere secluded."

Swift gave a brief nod and swiped away from the video on his phone to call the station. Annie trudged back over to where Jessica was still motionless on the bench.

"I'm sorry," Annie said, sitting down beside her. She opened her mouth to say more, but there was nothing to add that sounded genuine.

Jessica gave a curt laugh and stood up.

"It's okay," she said, her words clipped. "I'm just glad I got to see Oliver. Tell him I love him, won't you?"

"We've not given up on you, Jessica," Annie said. "We're going to find out who is doing this."

Jessica gave no inclination that she'd heard Annie. Wobbly on her feet, she headed towards the main road.

"Give me twenty minutes." She looked back over her shoulder at Annie. "I'll head to the disused site where we picked up that cat. There's a field next to it, away from the airport and away from people who matter. I'll wait there for you, or for whatever fate that is waiting for me."

Annie felt cold at the thought of Jessica dying out there alone.

"You're going to be okay," she shouted after her, but Jessica was gone between the parked cars. Annie turned her attention to her boss. "Swift, bring him in and let's do this."

FORTY-FIVE MINUTES LATER ANNIE AND SWIFT WERE sitting in an interview room opposite a young woman with cropped hair and a grin like she was chewing a wasp.

"I told you already," she said, butting her chin towards Annie. "Charge me with something or let me go."

She was tall, well built, but despite this, Annie felt annoyed at herself for not recognising the person in the video had been female. That may have made a difference to whether Jessica recognised them. Had she swayed Jessica in calling the target a male? The woman had no ID and was as tight lipped as a mafioso.

"As I've said on more than one occasion, miss, we've brought you in for your own safety." Swift was losing patience.

Annie too. The longer she was held in the station, the more chance their perp noticed that something was up, the less chance Jessica had of surviving to see the day out.

"Please can you just give us your name?" Annie asked, scouring the woman's face for a clue. And there was something, just a slight glimpse of recognition that had set Annie's senses whirring when she'd entered the room.

"I don't have to give you anything," she replied, well spoken, each word like a barb. "You lot have done little to help us, why the hell should I help you?"

Annie watched as she shuffled in her seat, a speck of emotion flickered across her face. *A way in.*

"What do you mean by we've done little to help you?" Annie inquired, gently.

The woman's eyes danced over Annie's, her forehead drawn.

"Nothing," she said, closing her mouth in a thin line.

Fingers of recognition were probing at Annie. The way the woman's nose had a slight tilted end, the vibrancy of her blonde hair, eyes just slightly too wide apart. Annie had seen this woman before, or at least, a version of this woman.

"Swift, will you excuse me for a moment?" Annie said, pushing her chair back and standing.

Swift put pause on the interview and stepped out behind Annie, motioning for the uniformed officer on the door to watch over their guest.

"What's up, O'Malley?" he asked as Annie sped through the corridor to their incident room.

Tink and Page were there, sifting through pages of paperwork, mug shots by the looks of them. Page looked up as Annie opened the door and headed to the noticeboards where all the photos were pinned.

"Sir," he said, putting down the picture of a petite brunette. "We've had the tox results in from Henry Chance's autopsy."

"And," Swift asked, palms on the table, taking his weight through his arms.

"Alpha-methylphenethylamine with a side dish of propanamide," Page said, crossing his hands behind his head and leaning back on his chair.

"Wait," Swift crossed the room in two steps and lifted the tox chart from the table. "That's almost exactly the same dosage as we saw in the poisoning of the pies."

"And not only that," Page added, like the proverbial cat with the cream. "We've linked that dosage to the death of a young boy last year, I'm waiting for the files to be brought over from county."

"So Henry Chance was killed by a toxic batch of

drugs, most likely deliberately contaminated." Swift puffed out his cheeks.

"And if I'm not mistaken," Annie added as the room quietened, her finger tapping the photograph of Henry on the noticeboard. "The girl we have in the interview room... she has got to be Henry's sister."

TWENTY

FOR A MOMENT, ANNIE COULDN'T MOVE. THE pictures and words written on the noticeboard swirled around in a kaleidoscope of confusion that centred on Jessica.

"Annie?"

She heard Swift calling her name, but she blocked him out, lifting a hand, asking for patience. Page and Tink had pulled up chairs and the room held its breath.

There was Jessica, right at the crux of this investigation. Attacked at her workplace and fitted with an explosive device that was genuine and terrifying. She was given tasks to perform; graffiti, lacing food with poison, stealing a pet, killing the pet, and now the killing of a person. But—and Annie didn't think she would have to dissect this case in such an odd way when there was a bomb in play—what if those tasks weren't just a distraction? What if there was more behind the graffiti and the poison, not just simple tools to make sure Jessica obeyed the rules? What if they weren't just the result of an evil, deranged mind, but of a clever one who'd thought out what and why Jessica was being asked to do them? If that was the case, then the interest was now not just with the people Jessica had put away, the ones who felt wronged by her, or the people who surrounded her every day. No, the focus needed to be on what Jessica had been asked to perform, and perhaps most importantly, why. She was a puppet in someone's sick game, but her puppet master was more Frankenstein than Geppetto, building a monster, a plaything, and making sure she was at his mercy.

"I think we've been looking at this all wrong," Annie said eventually, spinning and facing the table. "We've been trying to narrow down who Jessica has put away who might have links to the explosive or her old cases. What if we should have been looking at *what* she was asked to do? The tasks are more important than we've given them credit for."

"We are looking at them now there's imminent risk to a life," Page said.

"*Exactly*," Annie almost shouted, pointing a finger at Page. "Now we know the possible end point of the tasks, we're looking at the key figure involved. But we should have been doing that all along. We investigated the cans of spray and any acrostics or clues in the text, but did we really look into what the graffiti words meant? We looked at what the contaminant was in the shop, but did we really ask *why* those particular pies were poisoned? We managed to trap a stray cat, but did we ask why Jessica was asked to steal someone's pet and then kill it? No. We've been asking the wrong questions all this time. No wonder the perp has been way ahead of us, we're not looking in the right direction."

"But how do we know which direction to look in?" Tink said, lifting the pile of papers she'd been sifting through with Page before Annie and Swift had arrived. "There's so many loose ends and different strand to this case. There's not just the explosive and the tasks, there's the drugs, the fact Jessica is a prosecutor, the whole list of people she's put away. How do we know which of those strands is the *key* to putting a stop to all of this?"

"Oh God, I know." Annie pulled her hair out of its ponytail and drew it back up again, tighter, neater. "I think I'm nearly there; my brain is still trying to tie up all the ends."

"My brain hasn't even found the knotted part yet," Page joked, drawing his bottom lip into his mouth.

Annie took a breath and smiled at him. She could feel the energy seeping out of her body at its lack of sleep and food. But she knew they were all feeling the same. Page had put himself on the line by being in the shop when Jessica had contaminated the food. He'd protected people from death by standing not even a few feet from an explosive and noticing things that others didn't. DC Page had come up with the goods and he was well on the way to making his well-deserved sergeant's exam.

"You have," she said. "Think of everything you've done so far. Besides, you're the one who connected the amphetamines and the fentanyl from the pies to Henry Chance, and the death last year." The cogs that had been turning over and over in Annie's mind settled to a slow and dropped into place.

"That's it, isn't it?" Annie continued, her brain sparking. "I think *that's* the key to finding out who's at the end of all this. We need to find out how Jessica is linked to those drugs."

Annie turned back to the whole team, wide eyed and with a pinpoint clarity of what she needed to do.

"I think Jessica was chosen for a reason," she went on. "I think that the tasks were to exert power over her, control, make her feel as powerless as she made them feel. They were picked specifically for Jessica, and we need to know why. But I don't think the explosive is key. I think the drugs are."

"Henry Chance?" Swift asked.

"Yes," Annie pointed at him, on a roll now. "Henry Chance was being prosecuted for the murder of his partner, but he has previous arrest warrants for dealing drugs, not assault or battery or anything to suggest he was violent. In fact, most of the articles written about him spoke of what a nice guy he was. I'm not suggesting he was nice, quite the opposite given the nature of the girlfriend's death, but there was more to

178

Chance than that. And Chance died as a result of Jessica not being able to get to the courts. I mean, not directly, obviously there was a rather large link in between the two. I don't think Chance was killed because of what he did to his partner. I think he was killed because of the drugs. And *that* link is what we need"

"But how do we get it?" Swift wasn't asking Annie; he was asking himself.

"We go back to the beginning, and we find out who the young boy was who died last year," Page added, softly, not quite sure of himself.

"Exactly." Annie slumped into a chair, exhausted from the last few days of being alert and on the go.

"And I think I may be able to help you with that." All four of the MCU swung their attention in the direction of the door. DCI Robins stood there with a file gripped in her hands. "Good work, by the way, all of you. This is a tricky case and I appreciate your dedication to the cause. Late nights and weekends aren't for everyone. Not that you're given the option, of course."

Robins let out a laugh and Tink dropped her head onto the desk.

"You're not kidding," she muffled.

"You're one of the youngest here, DS Lock." Robins raised an immaculate eyebrow. "What's the matter, are you still hungover?"

"I wish," Tink muttered, her head still resting on the paperwork.

"What have you got there?" Swift asked, and Robins entered the room and handed him the file.

"The information on the drug deaths," she said. "As requested by young Page here."

Page beamed, his face lighting up as Swift handed the file over to him.

"Do the honours, Tom," he said.

Page lifted the flap on the file and pulled out a thick wad of papers. Robins left the room as silently as she arrived, leaving the MCU to get on with their case. The incident room hushed to a silence once again, fractured by the sounds of rustling papers.

"Blah, blah, died directly due to the misuse of illegal substances…" Page was reading from the sheet, picking out the parts he deemed important. "Blah, blah, blah, twenty years of age, white, male. Blah, blah, again an order of Alpha-methylphenethy-lamine with a side dish of propanamide, blah, bl…"

He stopped reading, his forehead creased, head tilted to one side.

"I recognise this name," he said, slowly, swinging his chair around to face the noticeboards. "Yes. Oh!"

"Page, please put us out of our misery," Tink piped up, trying to see over Page's arm to the name on the papers.

"The young, white male was Tyler Leek." Page stood from his chair and walked to where the photos dotted the blue cloth, unpinning one from the board he held it up for the team to see. "Younger brother of our snitch, Alfie."

"What?" Annie stuttered. "That little jerk."

She was angry that he had pulled the wool over her eyes. Angry that she'd almost felt sorry for him.

"No wonder he knew about our case," she went on. "Do you think he blamed Hart to stall us and lead us astray? Or just so he could be in the limelight."

"Maybe Hart does have something to do with this," Tink said.

Annie shook her head; it didn't feel right. But she faltered, not wanting to dish out feelings and hunches as though they were facts. Not wanting to be wrong again. Swift's eyes were on her, she could tell he knew she was holding back. He knew her, sometimes, better than she knew herself.

"Maybe," she said, eventually, neither confirming nor denying her real thoughts.

Swift jumped up to his feet, gathering his stuff and sweeping it into his bag.

"Page, get to the prison. I want a full search of Alfie's room and his person. Check his phone logs and his post," he said. "Check visitor logs, check his real relationship with Luke Hart, and check his record again. Tink, get back into the interview room with whoever it is we picked up and try and get the truth out of her. If she's Henry's sister then she needs to talk fast if she wants our help. Annie, you're with me, we're going to find Jessica and get her to be honest with us about why she was picked to be the martyr."

TWENTY-ONE

SWIFT PUT HIS FOOT DOWN AND SPED BACK TOWARDS the airport and the scrubland behind it.

"So you think the Shakespeare had more to it than simply being a blot on the bandstand?" he asked Annie.

"I think it could do." Annie held on to the door with one hand, searching her phone with the other, her head spinning as though she was on a roller coaster with the impetus of Swift's driving and not looking out the window. "Listen to this. Titus Andronicus is one of Shakespeare's less loved tragedies due in part to its graphic violence."

They spun over a roundabout and Annie felt her stomach lurch.

"Sorry," Swift said, not sounding very sorry.

"It's a revenge tragedy," Annie went on, taking a deep breath. "Littered with violence and themes of grief and mourning. I think that's why it was picked."

"The graphic violence?" Swift asked.

"No, though I think that was part of his thinking; there are Shakespeare tragedies without the violence so why pick Titus Andronicus?" Annie shook her head. "But, I think that the theme of revenge and grief is important, and maybe the graphic violence was a nod to what *could* happen if Jessica disobeyed him?"

"So someone who is in mourning, grieving, and who wants revenge?" Swift broke down what Annie was saying. "Fingers are all pointing in the direction of Alfie and his dead brother Tyler now, aren't they?"

"But I don't get why Alfie chose Jessica to be the pawn in his game," Annie said, scrolling the Wiki page for more information. "And who is he working with on the outside? Someone must be leaving the stuff for Jessica, the cans of spray paint, the contaminated drugs."

"Someone wrapped her in the bomb vest too," Swift added, drawing the car up onto the verge and killing the engine. "But that will have to wait. We need to talk to Jessica again, find out what she knows about Alfie."

"What about his file," Annie asked, jumping down from the car.

"Tech team are on it." Swift beeped the door locked and they took off over the gate and across the scrubland to the field.

There wasn't a soul in site. But the darting activity of the bats flickering over their heads, brought out by the encroaching dusk, made Annie feel as though someone was watching her. She felt their movement, turning to see them, but they were too quick. She shuddered and sped up, Swift right by her side.

"Where did she say she'd be?" he asked her, his head sweeping back and forth to try and catch sight.

"She said there was a field behind this scrub, far enough away from the airport," Annie replied.

Neither of them needed to add why Jessica needed to be far enough away from the planes roaring to the sky, packed with holiday makers off to Minorca, and workers off to catch their connecting flights in Amsterdam.

"Do you think I made the wrong call?" Swift asked. "Sending Jessica out on her own."

"No," Annie said, quickly. "You made a very difficult call, but your role is to protect people, and you were risk assessing. It's not exactly a situation you come across every day, is it? How can you plan for this kind of event? I'm sorry I shouted at you before. I know you're doing the best you can."

"You're kind," Swift said. "I think we'll chalk it down to experience and have to learn from it."

"My kindness?" Annie asked, confused.

Swift laughed, a heartfelt relief in the tightness of the evening. "No O'Malley, not your kindness. My decision making."

"Oh, yeah," Annie laughed too, glad she had Swift with her this time.

The scrubland was fading to blackness as the sun

set, and the sounds of animals scratching nearby echoed across the gloom. They passed by a washing machine, dumped there because it no longer worked, Annie assumed. Its door was flung open like a gaping mouth, the drum no longer metallic but a blood red with rust. Something scuttled across the ground in front of them making Annie skip to the side, startled, landing on Swift's toes.

"You okay?" he asked, grabbing her elbow and keeping her upright.

Annie could feel his pulse racing through his fingers.

"You're as afraid as I am, aren't you?" she asked, stopping to let her heart rate decrease.

Swift looked at her, his eyes fixed on hers.

"Probably more." His voice croaked, and he cleared his throat. "Do you think we should announce ourselves?"

They'd reached the end of the scrubland; another gate protected them from the field beyond. It glinted in the almost darkness, reflecting the light from the waning moon.

"Might be for the best," Annie agreed, walking to the gate, and looking past the hedgerow for signs of Jessica. "We don't want to startle her."

"Jessica?" Swift shouted.

Annie's blood ran cold through her veins. Though she had known it was coming, Swift's shout cut through the night like a bullet. All at once, Annie didn't want to announce they were there, she wanted to creep away, unseen, unheard, and climb onto her camp bed and cuddle Sunday. She glanced at Swift as he jumped the gate.

"Jessica?" Swift shouted again. "It's O'Malley and Swift. Can you make yourself known?"

Annie held onto the top rail, cold under her hands, and waited for the shout from Jessica.

There was nothing except the hoot of an owl.

"Jessica?" Swift started walking into the field.

Annie climbed the gate, her shoes slippery on the metal rungs. She gripped tightly with her hands and swung her legs over the bar, feeling the rust grip at the material of her trousers and threaten to upturn her. Jumping down the other side, Annie let out a gasp of air and called out to Jessica herself.

"It's dark out, Jessica," she shouted. "Can you let us know where you are?"

No reply.

Fingers of doubt started to crawl up Annie's neck and tickle her hair. Her scalp tightened and she felt her arms raise with goose bumps.

"Swift," she said, quieter now. "I don't like this."

Swift had stopped next to Annie, the warmth of his skin a comfort through her sleeves.

"Me neither," he whispered. "Would there be any reason for Jessica to lie about where she was going?"

Annie had hoped he wouldn't ask her that. "Only about a million and one."

Swift scoffed.

"She might want to wreak her own revenge. Or go somewhere and try to take the vest off herself. Especially now she's seen Oliver and knows he's okay. Maybe she got here and thought she was too close to other people?"

Annie scuffed the ground with her toe, pulling out her phone.

"I'm going to try and call the mobile."

"Woah," Swift held out his hands. "Is that a good idea? What if your call triggers the... you know?"

He made a noise like a small explosion, hand movements and all.

"I'm not sure that's how it works, is it?" Annie said, her fingers hovering over the call button on Jessica's name. "The perp started off by calling her mobile, before he moved to texts, didn't he?"

"Maybe just text then," Swift said, quickly. "Just in case she's out there having a nap and can't hear us. Or the perp is texting because he's triggered the call function somehow."

"Okay," Annie replied. "What should I say?"

Swift cocked his head at her.

"Not sure that matters all that much, does it?"

"If she's scared and awaiting news about the little scrote we've got locked up in an interview room to keep them safe, then I'd say it probably matters quite a bit."

"Fair enough." Swift bowed his head in defeat.

"How about *it's Annie, I'm at the field, where are you?*"

"Straight to the point," Swift agreed. "Unlike you."

Annie could hear the smile in his words, even if the dusk was now too dark to see it.

"Not funny, Joe," Annie replied, her voice shaking as much as her hands as she typed the message.

The text swooped away into the ether. Moments later the grass a few yards away lit up like a miniature football pitch.

What?

Annie sped towards the light, not wanting it to vanish before she got there. There, lying in the uncut grass, was a phone. And Annie didn't need to pick it up and open it to know who it belonged to.

"Swift." Annie's blood ran cold as she gathered it up in her hands, not daring to press the home button to illuminate the screen again.

"Jessica's?"

Annie nodded before realising just how dark it had gotten.

"Yes," she said, quietly. "Where is she?"

"I guess the best place to look would be her messages?" Swift posed it as a question, but Annie knew as well as Swift did that her messages could lead them to a lot more than Jessica's whereabouts. They could lead to another task. A task that Jessica could not do. A task that Jessica had run away from.

Annie held the phone in her outstretched palms. It was weighty, solid, unlike the phone in her own pocket.

"I don't want to touch it any more than I have done," she said. "What if there are fingerprints on it? What if I open it and set the bomb off?"

Swift wrapped his hands around Annie's, warm and strong.

"Fingerprints will be useless to us now," he said. "They'll all be Jessica's. And how else will we find out where she has gone? We need to take that risk. But I don't want you doing something that doesn't feel right."

He peeled his hands away, the phone wrapped in them, and tilted it to his face. The light from the screen lit Swift from below, sending shadows sweeping up past his forehead.

"Not locked," he muttered, clicking the buttons.

And, in the stillness of the evening, as the bats fluttered overhead and the nocturnal creatures started scouring for food, the air trilled with the sharp ringing of a phone. Annie felt her stomach fall through her body, reaching out to grab at Swift's arms to stop herself from toppling to the ground.

"Crap," Swift swore, jolting Jessica's phone from his hand so hard it dropped to the ground too.

He fumbled in his pocket and pulled out the source of the ringing, hitting answer.

"Page," he said, the loudness of his voice making Annie shiver. "This had better be good."

Annie could hear Page through the speaker pressed against Swift's ear. He was tinny and quick, but that didn't make his words any less chilling.

"Swift," he said. "It's Alfie Leek. He was sent to jail last year and, get this, he was denied bail, so he was incarcerated when his brother died."

"Who was his prosecutor?" Annie asked, her mouth close to Swift's so Page could hear her.

"I think you can probably guess that, O'Malley," Page answered. "It was Jessica. But, and this is where it gets interesting, Alfie's visitor logs show he's been getting a regular visitor."

"Who?" Swift demanded.

"Erinn Frampton."

"Jessica's sister?" Annie was stumped. "Why?"

"We've found a mobile phone stashed in his cell, tech are trying to get into it. And there's a team tracking down the younger sister as we speak."

"Great work, Page," Swift said. "Update as soon as you have one, please?"

He hung up the phone and plunged them both into darkness.

"So Erinn is working with Alfie?" Annie spoke her theories out into the open. "That's me thrown twice in the space of just a few hours. But she seemed so worried about Jessica when we were at the apartment. That's some good acting. God, what is going on."

"Help me find Jessica's phone, again, Annie." Swift's voice sounded like he was already on the ground, searching.

Annie tapped out a quick message to Jessica's phone and waited for it to illuminate the way. It shone straight into Swift's face, on his hands and knees grappling with the uneven grass. Pushing himself up, he clicked at the keys. Annie sidled closer to him to see what secrets were held in the palm of Swift's hand.

Each message was separated from the others, as though sent from differing phones. Swift started at the beginning, reading the instructions for the graffiti, where to find the spray paint, which building to vandalise.

"He must have sent messages as well as calling to start with. I wonder why he stopped calling. Skip to the end, Swift," Annie said, her fingers itching to steal the phone out from under his nose.

Swift clicked out of the message and scrolled down with excruciating slowness that had nothing to do with his dexterity, more to do with the age of the phone.

"There." Annie pointed at the most recent message and Swift clicked in to read it.

Annie couldn't move.

The words hit her like a punch to her stomach, she doubled over, retching onto the grass.

"Annie," Swift spoke softly and clearly, taking Annie's arm and hauling her upright. "It's going to be okay, but we need to move. Now."

She nodded, unable to speak, the words of the last message circling through her soul.

You failed. My family suffered at your hands, now yours will too.

One last chance to redeem yourself or I go after your son.

Go to 185 West Park Avenue. Find Mim O'Malley. Kill her.

TWENTY-TWO

"WHY MIM?" ANNIE SHOUTED OVER THE ROAR OF the engine. "What does my sister have to do with all of this?"

The adrenaline had taken over and Annie was talking nineteen to the dozen as Swift put his foot down and sped back to the city. They'd called for backup, but their ETA was over forty-five minutes and both Annie and Swift knew that was too long. Mim's rental house was to the south, the opposite direction to the airport, and they had no idea how much of a head start Jessica had.

Annie scanned the roads, searching for something, anything useful.

"She hasn't taken her car, though, has she?" Annie went on, the conversation changing direction as quickly as Swift was.

"Not that we know," Swift yelled over the

honking of a car horn and the screeching of brakes. "But desperate people will do desperate things."

Annie felt sick.

Swift buzzed the radio in the car.

"Control, it's DI Swift," he said, giving his call number. "Can you search for any car jackings, auto thefts, anything like that from today. The last couple of hours even. Send details to my mobile, asap. Thanks."

He hit the radio off and put both hands back on the wheel, his knuckles white with the force of his grip.

"Swift?" Annie wanted to ask him a million questions but none of them would form correctly in her mouth.

"It's okay, Annie." Swift sped up, forcing her back into her chair. "It's going to be okay."

But when they sped into the cul-de-sac where Mim was staying, it wasn't okay. An old, battered Ford had mounted the pavement, two wheels on it, two wheels hanging off. The door was still open, swinging on its hinges like a loose tooth. Swift pulled up behind it and killed the engine.

"Looks like she's here already," he said, jumping down from the car.

Annie could barely move her arms to open the door. Everything was in slow motion, a thick sludge around her slowed her movements and made everything hurt. She braced her feet on the edge of the doorframe and slid down into Swift's arms.

"What if after all this time Mim ends up dead because of me?" she sobbed.

"Don't think like that," Swift said, pushing the door shut behind her. "Come on, with me."

The house was dark, the curtains shut. Swift and Annie crouched low and hopped over the garden wall. On the move, now, Annie felt a sense of purpose that made her move on autopilot. She had to be strong for her sister or she'd be a hindrance.

"This way," Swift hissed.

He circled the neat borders, careful not to trample the flowers and ran to the corner of the house, Annie was right on his heels, daring not to breathe. They stopped and as Swift ducked his head around the corner, Annie heard voices—shouts, high pitched and petrified.

Mim.

Swift motioned to Annie to follow, and they crept around the side of the house to the back garden. A light seeped out from one of the downstairs windows, pooling on the Astro turf making it a sickly green.

"There," he whispered, pointing at a window in the room next to the light.

Annie crept underneath it and bobbed her head up slowly. The room was empty though it looked like Mim had set up an office. Through the gloom Annie could see a small desk and piles of books. She gave the window a gentle tug, hoping with everything she had that it wasn't on a child lock and would open more than the few inches it already was.

It gave in her hands, opening towards her as though it had been recently oiled. Annie pulled herself up on the ledge and lifted her feet off the ground.

"No way." Swift circled behind her and lifted her away from the window.

Annie kicked out, silently, mad at him for what he had done.

"Joe," she hissed. "Mim is my sister."

"Exactly," he hissed back. "You're running on fumes, Annie. You're panicked and scared."

Annie felt like hitting him.

"And you're not?" she asked.

"Look," he whispered, levering himself onto the windowsill. "This is too dangerous; I can't let you into the house in all good conscience. I'd never forgive myself if something happened to you."

"But what about you?" Annie replied, her heart beating hard in her throat.

"I'm going to go and assess the situation," he whispered, running a hand down Annie's cheek. "And I'm going to save your sister."

"Thank you." Annie felt tears where Swift's hand had been, tickling her skin. "Be careful."

Swift disappeared into the window and Annie ducked to the ground, back against the wall, trying not to sob.

The voices grew louder, echoing across the dark garden. Sucking in her tears, Annie rose to her feet and walked slowly to the source of light. She didn't have a weapon with her, but Annie knew if she was in the same room as Jessica, she would fight with her bare hands to save Mim. Swift had been right, Annie couldn't separate work from family right now, no matter how much she wanted to.

Beyond a narrow gap in the curtains, Annie could see Mim huddled in the corner of her new sofa. Incongruous against the vibrant pink, Mim was a shell of herself. She glanced around the room as best she could and caught sight of Jessica, stalking the room, a large knife in her hands.

The woman was pacing. Up and down the back wall, out of sight of Mim, the knife handle gripped tightly in her fingers. She was muttering something that Annie couldn't make out, but the steely look on her face made bile rise in Annie's throat.

Come on, Swift.

"Why are you doing this?" Mim's voice broke, and Annie broke with it. "Please just let me go. I'll promise never to tell anyone. Is this because of my mum? Are you working for her?"

Annie stopped breathing, not believing what she was hearing. She strained to hear Jessica's reply over her pulse.

"I don't know who the hell you are," Jessica spat. "Just stop talking to me."

"Then what are you doing here?" Mim asked. "Why me?"

"Look." Jessica was angry, she powered over to the sofa and stood over Mim. "Your sister made sure

197

that the first target is now safe. I can't get to them anymore. So now you're revenge."

"Annie?" Mim asked. "Revenge for what?"

"I don't bloody know, do I?" Jessica shouted, pacing in front of the sofa now, the knife glinting in the light. "I just do as I'm told."

"But surely you can ask for protection too?" Mim whimpered as Jessica leant over her, the knife near her throat. "If Annie helped the other person, she can help you too. She's a good person, please, and so am I."

Annie's eyes filled with tears; she blinked them away hurriedly, not wanting to miss a moment.

"No one can help me. Look." Jessica pulled open the coat she was wearing, giving Mim a full view of the explosive vest.

"Oh god, oh god, please leave me alone." Mim drew herself as small as possible into the sofa.

Annie wanted to climb in the window, to grab hold of Jessica and smother herself around the explosive so it didn't harm her sister.

"I didn't want to hurt anyone," Jessica went on, twisting the knife around in her hands, practising a few sudden movements. "I don't know how I'm going to do this. But I promise to make it as quick as I can."

"Please." Mim's sobs wrenched at Annie's heart and stoked at an anger inside her that pulsed in her eyes.

"I can't." Jessica was crying now, her hands shaking. "You have to understand, my boy, my Oliver, he's in danger if I don't follow my orders."

"Then get him to safety too," Mim cried.

"It's too late." Jessica grabbed Mim's arm and dragged her to her feet.

From the window, Mim looked diminutive, smaller than Annie remembered her being because her nature was to be big and proud and loud. But up against Jessica, she looked like a child. The older woman pushed Mim up against the wall, her forearm to Mim's neck. Annie could see the blood start to pool in her face, turning it from pale to purple. She grabbed the window and tugged at it, willing it to open.

Beyond the curtain, Swift ran into the room and pushed Jessica away from Mim, the knife rolling across the floorboards and clattering under an armchair. Mim groaned and fell to her knees, clutching at her throat. Jessica cried out, regaining her balance, her gaze steely on Swift. Annie took the moment of confusion to wrench the widow wide and drag herself inside. She didn't care what Swift said, she had to get to her sister.

"Annie," Swift yelled. "Grab Mim and get her to safety. Out the front door, I've just unlocked it. Go. Now. Quick."

Annie didn't need to be told twice. She ran across the room to Mim and dragged her up by the elbow. Forcing Mim's arm over her shoulders, Annie bypassed Swift, her sister as light as a feather, as they made their way towards the hallway.

"Get out," Swift whispered to Annie as they passed him. "Go as far as you can. And when the backup gets here, get the area cleared as quickly as possible."

"I'll do it," Annie cried. "Come on, Swift, you too."

Swift shook his head.

"I need to make sure you're out and okay before I leave Jessica alone."

"Swift!"

Annie tried to plead with him, but he pushed her out of the living room and slammed the door shut behind her.

"Quickly, Mim," Annie whispered to her sister, feeling another sob rise in her throat. "This way."

They ran to the front door, the latches unlocked as promised, and pulled it open.

And there, standing just on the other side looking like a ghost, was Erinn.

TWENTY-THREE

"WHERE IS SHE?" ERINN'S EYES WERE HUGE, DARK, and full of something primal that made Annie's hair stand on end.

She's dangerous.

Annie moved in front of Mim, protecting her with her body. She balled her hands into fists, trying to hide the way they were shaking.

"Erinn," Annie said, gently, trying to coax her away from the doorway. "Jessica is with the police now. They're looking after her. She'll be okay. I need you to step outside so we can secure the area."

Annie hoped the tremor in her voice would be less noticeable if she sounded confident.

"The police?" Erinn's face twisted into a grin. "Where are the cars? The flashing blue lights? You mean you and that old guy you were with? Hardly *the police* now, are you? You can't stop me."

Annie grabbed out at the door with her hand, stepping back, pushing into Mim who stumbled and reached out for Annie's shoulders. But Erinn was too quick, spotting what Annie was trying to do and forcing her foot onto the door frame, jamming it open.

"Erinn, please," Annie cried out, swinging the door closed as far as it would go. It bounced back, hitting Erinn's foot. "Your sister is in danger, you are too. We need to get out of here and let Swift do what he's best at."

"What he's best at?" Erinn said, wrenching the door painfully out of Annie's fingers. "You mean wrangling cats and trying to look mean. Give me a break."

Drawing her hands back, Annie felt the sharp pain of her fingernail bending too far, ripping away from the nail bed. She gasped, feeling the sting run down her finger and into her hand. Erinn used the distraction to step forwards into the house and push Annie out of the way. Annie grappled thin air for something to get purchase on, a wall, a door, anything. Her fingers whacked against a table, sending a second shock of pain down her wrists, but she gripped tightly and recovered her balance. It was too late though; Erinn strode towards the living room door and swung it open.

"Jessica," she screamed, and the air around Annie turned to ice.

Annie felt something wrap around her hands, pulling her towards the front door.

"Come on, Annie," Mim said, pulling harder. "We need to get out of here."

Annie looked between her sister, the wonderful person she was taking time to get to know, and the living room, shaking her head.

"I can't leave him in there with two of them," Annie said, peeling her hands from Mim's. "You go, wait for the police, and let them know what's happened. They shouldn't be long now. Go, quickly."

Mim faltered in the doorway, her eyes dark.

"No, Annie, please." Mim shook her head. "Come with me."

But Annie had made up her mind. It wasn't fair to leave Swift to deal with this on his own. Annie was his partner, and she was going to act like one.

"I'll be fine, Mim," Annie called, running back into the house. "Go."

Not looking behind her, Annie burst through the door into the living room. Swift was by the front window, staring into the room. Annie looked to what had his attention and saw Erinn, her arms wrapped around Jessica.

"Oh Jess." She was sobbing, full throaty sobs that made her whole-body shake. "I'm so sorry."

Annie took a step towards them, not knowing how fragile the explosives were, not knowing if Erinn's hugs would set them off.

"O'Malley," Swift said, sternly. "What are you doing in here, I thought I told you to get out."

Annie moved to Swift's side, her eyes not leaving the sisters.

"I tried," she said, nodding at the two girls wrapped in each other's arms. "But someone got in my way. Besides, I can't leave you to get all the credit now, can I?"

She was trying to joke, but with each slight movement from Erinn, Annie felt her heart wobble in her chest.

"What's going on?" Annie went on. "From the look on her face when she pushed past me, I thought Erinn was here for blood."

"Are you okay?" Swift asked. "Did she hurt you?"

"I'm fine," Annie whispered, aware of the changing feeling in the room now her heart wasn't beating quite so loudly in her ears. "Thank you for asking."

Swift nodded once and they both turned their attention back to the sisters.

"I didn't know it would be like this," Erinn mumbled into Jessica's shoulder. "I thought he was going to get you to do a few stupid things to make you feel bad for putting him away. Throw pebbles at cars or tip over people's bins. I never thought it would be so dangerous."

Jessica struggled to free herself from Erinn's grip, she held her out at arms' length, her hands on her younger sister's shoulders.

"What do you mean?" Jessica hissed. "You thought *who* would make me tip over a bin?"

Erinn dropped her arms; tears fell to the floor as she sniffed and muttered something that was neither audible nor visible.

"Alfie Leek," Swift interrupted. "Erinn has been visiting Alfie Leek in prison, we think that's who is behind all of this."

"What?" Jessica looked incensed, her eyes wild. "Have you been selling drugs for Alfie?"

Annie thought that was a weird first question, but she kept her mouth shut. Jessica was used to prosecuting those who thought drugs were a good way of life, she was probably just worried about her sister falling into the wrong crowds.

"No." Erinn shook her head so hard the hair around her face fell free of its band. "Of course I haven't. I just felt sorry for him, that's all. What with his brother and all."

"Alfie is an idiot, Erinn," Jessica shouted. "How are you in contact with him? I don't understand."

"He used to write to me, when he first got sent away and I threw all those letters in the bin because he said he'd seen me on your social media and thought I was pretty," Erinn sniffed. "I thought he was a creep. But then he seemed to change. He talked about how much he missed Tyler and I, sort of, wrote back... I'm sorry."

Jessica threw her arms into the air and let out a cry of frustration.

"What were you thinking?" She was pacing again, Erinn watching on with a scared look on her face.

"This is my fault; I knew I shouldn't have stayed close to you all when I started this job. I get used to all the nutters I put on trial, but it's not fair to get you involved too."

Erinn put her hands on her hips and jutted out her chin.

"I'm not a child," she said, looking exactly like a child having a tantrum. "I can make my own decisions. Alfie just wanted to get you back for the death of his brother."

"I didn't kill his brother," Jessica spat at Erinn. "He died *when* Alfie was in jail, not *because* Alfie was in jail. And it was all on Alfie, I didn't make him sell drugs, did I? Don't you see? He's been manipulating you. I bet he made out like he'd be a great boyfriend because you'd always know where he was, didn't he? He's a smooth talker, I'll give him that. He tried that with me too. Knob."

Erinn's face lit up like a stop sign and Annie thought back to how Erinn dissed Jessica's ex because he was out in all hours unlike her own. Annie had thought Jessica's ex had been the dodgy one but working shifts in a hospital was a darn sight better than being stuck in jail.

"Shut up," Erinn hissed, drawing herself upright and puffing out her chest. "You just shut up. You know, I said yes to Alfie's stupid plan because I wanted to get back at you for making me always feel inferior to you. You think you're so clever, yet who's the one here strapped up with a load of crap to your chest."

"The Shakespeare?" Annie gasped. "It's revenge, but it's *your* revenge isn't it, Erinn? Titus Andronicus was about brothers; you picked the tasks?"

Erinn shrugged, her face twisted. "Not all of them, no. But the addition of that particular piece of text was my idea. Did you enjoy it?"

"It's not his best work," Annie pressed.

"You can shut up too," Erinn scoffed and turned her attention back to Jessica.

"The pies and the cat?" Jessica said, her voice shaking. "We used to share those pies when Mum and Dad argued and neither of them could be bothered to make us dinner. I've just remembered that. I used to steal them after school, and we'd break them in half and eat them on the way home. Why those? And why make me kill a cat?"

Erinn slumped forwards, her body bending at the waist. She let out a keen so soul puncturing it made Annie's skin crawl. Erinn dropped to her knees, gripping Jessica's ankles.

"I wanted you to know it was me," she started sobbing again. "I wanted you to think of me when you were doing them, to know how angry I was with you. It was Alfie's idea, and I believed him, believed that we could both get back at you for how you had wronged us. And then he asked you to kill the cat and I knew something was going really wrong. I told him to stop, I didn't want anything else to do with it, but he just took over the tasks. I never wanted anyone to get hurt. It's not even a real vest, is it? It's just pretend. It's all just pretend."

Erinn was on her feet, scrambling up Jessica's legs. She pulled at her coat, tearing it off Jessica's arms with surprising force and began to tug at the vest. Jessica tried to fight back, to hold her arms to her chest, but after three days of no sleep and very little food, she was weak and tired.

"Stop, Erinn, stop," Swift shouted, but Erinn was fixated on what she was doing.

Erinn spun her sister around, unzipping the vest where it was attached at Jessica's back. She pushed her sister to the sofa, grabbing the vest in her hands as the other woman fell.

"It's all a lie," Erinn sobbed. "I would never hurt anyone. I promise I wouldn't."

Jessica screamed, kicking out with her feet to try and right herself. Annie could see the mechanisms of the explosive poking out the bottom of the vest that Erinn was waving maniacally around.

"Erinn, it's real, it's not a fake," Annie cried. "Put it down and step away. Jessica get out."

Jessica didn't need telling twice. She slid onto the floor and pulled herself away from her sister.

"Annie, run," Swift yelled, pushing her towards the living room door, losing his footing and skidding to his knees.

Annie jolted to the door and felt a hand around her arm.

"Annie, quick." It was Mim, she grabbed Annie and pulled her out of the door into the hallway with Jessica.

She slammed it shut behind them and dragged Annie to the front door.

"SWIFT!" Annie shouted, not able to get the vision of Swift sacrificing himself to save her out of her mind. "Let me go."

Annie wriggled in Mim's arms, not able to break free.

The cold of the night hit her smack bang in the face. Blue lights lit up the road and the steady beat made Annie feel sick. Strong hands lifted her away from Mim and away from the house.

And the air was filled with the sounds of the explosion.

TWENTY-FOUR

THE WORLD TILTED ON ITS AXIS.

Annie felt herself thrown into the ether and suspended there, though her feet were still firmly on the ground. A cacophony of noise erupted around her, but Annie felt like she was trapped in a bubble. She swallowed, trying to unblock her ears.

Swift.

Annie remembered the way he'd pushed her towards safety, making sure she was okay before himself. And Mim, she had come back inside to help her. Annie felt red, hot bile rise in her chest, stinging her throat. She doubled over, swallowing again, not wanting to throw up in the middle of the street. It was her fault that Mim had come back in, her fault that Swift had to save her and not himself. Annie had made the decision to go back inside the house and look where it had left them.

She pushed herself up straight and started running

back towards the open front door. Strong arms clad in a fireproof jacket swung to catch her and hold her back.

"Let me go," she yelled, her eyes scanning the darkened front door for signs of life.

She couldn't see anything. The smoke billowing out blocked her view. The windows of the living room were scattered across the front lawn. Broken glass sparkled in the flashing blue lights of the police cars and fire engines, dotting the petals of the early bluebells.

"Can't do that, Miss," the fireman holding her back said. "We need to check the building is secure. There could be more explosive ready to go off."

"But my…"

What was Swift? Her boss, her DI…

"My *friend* is trapped in there," she shouted, struggling against the fireman. "He could be hurt. Please you have to let me go to him. I'm police."

"You could be Father Christmas and I'd still say no," the fireman replied.

He hauled Annie off her feet and took her back to the pavement, handing her over to a small huddle of people who wrapped their arms around Annie and coaxed her to a stillness.

"It's going to be okay." Annie recognised Tink's voice.

"He's strong." That one was Page.

"And resourceful." Even DCI Robins was there.

Annie pulled herself out of Page's clutches and

looked at her team, the people who she'd grown so fond of in just over a year. They'd taken Annie into their folds and treated her with respect and kindness and look how she'd repaid them.

"I'm so sorry," she whimpered, her eyes blurry with tears. "I shouldn't have let him go in. *I* shouldn't have gone in."

"You think you could have stopped him?" Tink asked, taking Annie's hand. "When Swift gets an idea in his head, he's like a carthorse, nothing can stop him."

"But he saved me, and then he slipped over." Annie couldn't keep it in anymore. Her whole body clenched with the guilt. "If I hadn't been there, he might have gotten out."

"If you hadn't been there," Tink replied, squeezing Annie's fingers. "Swift would have been rescuing someone else."

"If you hadn't been there," Robins added. "Jessica would have been taken out by our ERU three days ago."

"If you hadn't been there." It was Page's go now. "Sunday would still be living feral under a hedge."

Annie spluttered out a laugh, wiping her face with her sleeve, she sniffed and smiled at her team.

"You guys are the best," she said, hiccupping away more tears.

From the house, the sounds of splintering wood and smashing glass silenced them. Annie spun around just in time to see the front wall of the living room collapse in on itself in a cloud of brick dust and smoke. The firefighters shouted instructions and moved their workers back, the stream of water still jettisoning into the ever-growing flames.

Annie didn't think twice. Ignoring the shouts of her team, she double backed on the crowds, running as fast as she could to the neighbouring property. Hopping the fence and circling towards their back gardens, Annie couldn't see for tears, she couldn't think for the racing panic that muddled her brain.

"Swift," she shouted, aimlessly because even without the sounds of the water and the fire and all the people there watching the catastrophic events unfold, she was too far away from Mim's rental for him to hear. "Swift!"

Annie reached the fence separating the two gardens. Caring not about the brambles that clutched at her legs or the holly bush that scratched at her face, Annie clambered over the fence and landed with a thud in her sister's garden.

"Joe," she shouted again. "Where are you?"

Smoke bellowed out of the open window where Annie herself had climbed in only moments earlier. The glass here was still intact, the walls still upright. Annie ran to the window, pulling her jumper up to cover her mouth and stave off the acrid smoke that hit the back of her throat. She couldn't see past the smoke. Couldn't hear anything over the fire that was raging at the front of the room.

"Shit," Annie swore, looking around for someone to help.

But she was all alone in the garden. The only person who could help was her. She gathered herself and took a great gulp of fresh air, ducking back to the window and hauling herself in.

It was dark, too dark to make out anything other than the flames licking at what was left of the curtains. Annie fell to her knees and spread out her hands, feeling for Swift or Erinn.

She tried to call out, but the smoke was too strong. Pulling her jumper back over her mouth, Annie kept feeling along the floor until her fingers hit something malleable.

Swift.

Annie felt her way across the object, palpating the fabric and what was underneath. The bony shin. The curves of a knee. It was a leg. She gripped the ankle with one hand, feeling around for another, and then heaved the body towards the window with all her might. Feeling lightheaded with the smoke, her eyes stung, her mouth felt like the inside of a lit cigarette. Annie coughed into her jumper. Just a few more feet.

A creaking noise made her whimper. The ceiling had started to collapse. Pieces of plaster and wood rained down onto Annie's head. They rained down onto the fire, stoking the flames into a beast that started licking towards Annie.

"Come on," she yelled, mostly at herself, as she

leant all her weight towards the window and her escape. "COME ON."

"Annie?" Page's voice shouted from out in the garden. "Bloody hell, O'Malley, what are you doing?"

"Where are you?" Tink cried.

"I've got him," she called out, her back hitting the wall. "Help me."

She threw an arm out of the window and felt around in the smoke for Tink and Page. Someone gripped their fingers through hers and she clung onto them like a life belt. Hauling herself through the window she collapsed onto the grass, coughing, choking, trying to point in the direction of Swift.

"In there," she croaked. "Get him out."

Page disappeared into the house, his feet the last thing to go. And the seconds that passed seemed like hours until his face popped up, and there tucked under his arms was DI Joe Swift. His face was blackened with soot, his arm bleeding and held at an awkward angle. But he was alive and breathing and Annie felt herself fold over with relief as the paramedics ran to their side.

ANNIE COULD TELL THAT, ONCE AGAIN, ROBINS WAS going to tear a strip off her. The DCI stood with her hands on her hips, glaring in Annie's direction where she sat at the doors of the ambulance. Annie's legs dangled over the edge of the open doors and next to her was Mim. Swift was laid out on a stretcher, his smoky face covered in an oxygen mask, his arm bandaged. Behind the ambulance, with a flurry of activity that had arrived days too late, were the EOD, shouting commands at their team while the rest of the emergency services looked on with raised brows.

"Thank you, O'Malley," Robins said, after a moment's deliberation. "For rescuing him."

"I would have been fine." Swift had lifted his mask and was trying not to laugh. A cough overcame him, and he slunk down onto the stretcher, O2 firmly back in place.

"I'm sorry," Annie said, looking at her toes. "For breaking the rules and going against what the firemen were saying. I just…"

Her voice choked in her throat, and it was nothing to do with the smoke inhalation that she was being shipped off to hospital for.

"It's okay," Robins said, stepping up to Annie and putting a hand on her knee. "I know."

They shared a moment, so brief that Annie could have imagined it. But the look in Robins' eyes would be one she remembered for years to come. Robins knew how Annie felt about Swift. Annie felt her cheeks heat and was glad of the interruption from Tink and Page.

"Local hero here, anyone need rescuing?" Page flexed his muscles and laughed.

Mim jumped down from the back of the ambulance and hugged Tink and Page together.

"Thank you for saving my sister," she said, her voice muffled in their coats. "One day she'll do as she's told and not get into so much trouble."

"I hope not," Swift coughed from his stretcher.

Annie leaned an arm around and squeezed his foot as a thanks.

"I hope you two have been given the all clear?" Robins asked Tink and Page. "We've still got work to do and these two reprobates are going to be out for the next few days."

Tink gave a salute and Page nodded sagely.

"Reporting for duty, sir... er ma'am." Tink laughed and dropped her hand from her head.

"Wait," Annie interrupted their chatter. "What do you mean *still work to be done*? Jessica is safe, isn't she? And Alfie's in jail already. And Erinn?"

Annie didn't want to know what had happened to the younger sister, with all the smoke and the collapsed wall and ceiling, it hadn't looked good.

"Erinn is on her way to the hospital. She's not in a great way, but she's alive." Page twisted his hands around. "She lost both arms when the vest went off."

"Oh god," Annie gasped, not able to imagine how heart breaking that would be for a young woman. "Poor thing."

"And Jessica is sitting in the back of a police car awaiting a talking to," Tink added.

"What?" Annie said. "Why? For leaving her apartment, or for going after Mim? I don't think a talking to is what she needs. She needs a hot bath and some food."

Tink and Page looked at each other and then back at Annie.

"What?" Annie asked.

"What's going on?" Swift was up on his elbows, trying to peer out the back of the ambulance.

"So," Tink started. "Jessica may have been on the receiving end of some nasty people. Alfie and Erinn were trying to get revenge for the death of Alfie's brother."

"Right," Annie agreed. "Alfie thought if he hadn't been in jail then he could have saved him?"

"Not quite." Tink took Mim's place and sat down next to Annie so Swift could lie down again and still hear her, sitting up was making him go a deep shade of purple. "Turns out that Alfie's brother was killed with a dodgy batch of drugs because he had been dealing on someone else's patch."

"I still don't get why that's Jessica's fault." Annie coughed, feeling weary.

"Because the patch belonged to Jessica." Tink nodded at Annie's surprise. "Henry Chance and his sister were working for Jessica. She told them to slip him some contaminated drugs."

"That's awful," Annie said, her mind whirring. "So that's why Alfie was so angry."

"Yep," Tink confirmed. "But it doesn't end there. Jessica was so good at putting away those dealers and so well revered in her job because she knew exactly who they were, so she could always incriminate them. Miss Chance gave us a list of people Jessica has convicted who also worked for her. She was so worried for her brother Henry because he had decided to go public and that's when his girlfriend was stabbed. Henry would have gone away for a very long time for something he didn't do. He sold drugs, but he never hurt anyone like that."

"So Jessica stabbed Henry's girlfriend?" Annie asked, her mouth gaping. "Just so he wouldn't blab."

"Apparently so," Tink said. "Though obviously we can't take Miss Chance's word for it. But it seems like Jessica was locking away her staff when they got too mouthy for her."

"Wow, you think you know someone." Annie leant her head back against the door of the ambulance and all of a sudden felt as though she could sleep for a year.

"Let's leave them to it," Robins said, steering her team and Mim away from the ambulance.

"Mim," Annie called before they'd gotten too far. "Stay at mine, you can look after Sunday until I'm released from the hospital."

Mim blew her a kiss and ran to catch up with the team. Page wrapped an arm around her shoulder and the four of them walked off into the flashing blue night.

"Come on then, O'Malley," Swift croaked from his bed. "Let's get somewhere warm and dry and preferably not on fire. I smell like a BBQ."

Annie climbed up into the ambulance and sat on the chair facing Swift. She took his hand in hers and leant back, shutting her eyes.

"I didn't mean what I said about being okay," Swift said, quietly. "You saved my life out there, Annie. Thank you."

"I couldn't let you get away with sacrificing yourself for me, now, could I?" she said, as the paramedic closed the doors. "You'd never let me hear the end of it."

TWENTY-FIVE

ONE WEEK LATER

"So let me get this straight," Mim said, tucking into a chunk of warm bread dipped in oil and vinegar. "Alfie Leek didn't actually know that Jessica was the head of the rival drug gang and called for the execution of his brother? He strapped her with a bomb just because she'd put him in jail and he missed out on the opportunity to save Tyler. Sheesh."

She whistled through her teeth and dunked her bread again, the dark balsamic spreading in bubbles through the golden olive oil.

Annie tore a chunk off the doughy loaf of focaccia and nibbled at the edges. They were sitting at the large table in Swift's kitchen as he whistled merrily at the stove.

"She's being charged with possession with the intent to sell, GBH, ABH, and manslaughter because apparently she didn't mean to kill Henry's girlfriend, just maim her a little," she said. "Yet we still don't know who originally strapped the bomb to Jessica's chest, or who made it. We're trying to get that information out of Alfie, and may have to use some of what Jessica did as leverage."

"God, imagine what Alfie would have done if he'd known Jessica was actually responsible for the death of Tyler." Mim tore off another handful of bread and stuffed it in her mouth as though she'd not eaten in a week. Talking behind her hands, she added, "are all the baddies you put away so... what word am I looking for... manipulative, crazy, dangerous? That's it, dangerous."

"Yep," Swift called from across the kitchen. "That's why we get them in the MCU. But I'm not sure they're called *baddies* anywhere other than on television."

"Cheeky," Mim called back. "It's a good job you can cook. This bread is amazing."

She swiped another chunk and dipped it in the mixture before turning to Annie and lowering her voice.

"So my sister is a bone fide bad ass, then?" she said, reaching out her oily fingers and clutching at Annie's. "You're so cool."

"I wouldn't go that far," Annie said, her throat

still stinging from the smoke, her lungs heavy. "We just do our job the best we can, like anyone else would."

"Shut up with your false modesty, you doofus." Mim slapped the top of Annie's hand and went back to her bread. "Your team is incredible. The way you went running in to rescue Swift, the way Tink and Page followed you into the breach. The way Swift pushed you out of harm's way. You *are* like something out of a tv show."

Her green eyes sparkled under her cropped fringe and Annie had the distinct feeling that Mim was about to ask to join them in battle.

"It's dangerous," Annie pre-empted. "We've been subjected to a crazy woman trying to steal children, a teenager killing her friends out of jealousy, the bloody plague. You're better off well away. You saw yourself, anyway, I don't know why I'm having to persuade you away from police work. A woman strapped with a bomb tried to slash your throat. If that's not enough to ward you off, I don't know what is?"

Mim glanced at Annie through her thick lashes.

"Yet you keep coming back for more," she said, her lips pulling into a cheeky grin. "I wonder why that is."

She sat back in her chair, lifting her red wine to her lips, and looking like the annoying little sister Annie remembered.

"Don't," Annie mouthed, feeling her cheeks heat, and reaching for her own glass.

"Supper is served." Swift appeared at the table with laden hands.

He proceeded to place down wonderful dishes full of beef bourguignon, dauphinoise potatoes, and teeny carrots with their green tops still attached. All served in a pinny with a hot looking smile.

"Jeez, Swift," Mim salivated. "You're wasted on the force. This is incredible."

"Thanks, Joe." Annie smiled at him, her stomach letting out a groan.

"Well, enjoy," he said, pulling the apron over his head and grabbing a dished plate from the island.

"Wait, you're not joining us?" Annie asked.

"Nope, not this evening." Swift popped a carrot in his mouth. "I thought you two might enjoy some time alone. I'm going to lounge on the sofa and watch *baddies* on tele."

"But you've spent all day preparing dinner," Annie added.

"And I'm still going to eat it," Swift smiled. "Don't worry about me, O'Malley, you and Mim have loads to catch up on. Like I said the other day, I'm happy to offer my space up if it means poor Mim isn't having to eat a microwave meal and get rickets."

"I eat well," Annie piped up.

"Pete feeds you well." Swift winked and headed out of the kitchen, closing the door softly behind him.

224

"Who is Pete and why is Swift not married?" Mim said, before the silence had settled.

"Pete is the pizza man who owns the cafe under my flat," Annie replied, taking a glug of wine.

She tucked into her food, ignoring the other question. The beef melted in her mouth and gave way to a complex aftertaste that was like something from the Gods. Maybe Swift was wasted in the force, he was certainly a top-notch chef.

Warmed with wine and food, Annie couldn't help but want to scratch the itch she'd been feeling since that night in the fire.

"You know when Jessica had you by the throat, with the knife and everything?" she started, pronging the last carrot with her fork and nibbling at the end of it.

"Mmhmm." Mim nodded, her mouth full.

"You asked if she had anything to do with our mum," Annie felt her throat constricting and took another sip of Malbec. "Why? Was our mum so awful to you and Dad that you would think her bad enough to come at you with an explosive and a knife?"

Mim took a moment, chewing slowly and looking into the distance through the closed curtains in Swift's kitchen. The large clock on the wall ticked loudly, somewhere in the house a water pipe clicked into life, gurgling in the walls, and rattling across the ceiling. Annie wiped the last of her food up with a mop of focaccia and sat back, full, and ready to hear the worst.

"Mum loves you," Mim started, wiping her mouth with her napkin. "She always did. I don't think she was quite so eager when I came along though. She was mixed up in some stuff that wasn't good for our family. Look, I think it's best that we have a proper conversation about what I've been told, but not here though."

She put down her cutlery and sat back, hands on her stomach.

"Why not here?" Annie asked. "Swift is miles away in the living room, trust me, he can't hear what we're saying."

"Then he won't be able to hear me say, you need to tell him how you feel, will he?" Mim laughed and Annie turned the colour of her wine.

"Keep on topic, please!" She winced at the idea that maybe Swift *could* hear them. "Talk to me about Mum."

"I will," Mim said, nodding. "And I've sorted something out for the both of us to talk properly to each other with no distractions. I think it will be a great way for us to get to know each other properly. I know we had planned a spa trip away, but then all this happened. So I have treated us to something even more exciting."

Her eyes glistened in the candlelight.

"What?" Annie asked, getting impatient.

"We're going to Spain." Mim clapped her hands together with glee. "One week in a posh hotel with sun, sea, and…"

"No more secrets?" Annie interrupted.

"No more secrets," Mim agreed.

"Sounds amazing, thank you, sign me up." Annie reached over and took Mim's hand.

"Already have," Mim smiled. "We leave on Monday."

READ ON

Read on for a sneak peek to see what O'Malley &
Swift are up to next...

Annie O'Malley & DI Swift return in ONE LAST
BREATH

**THE SEVENTH INSTALMENT IN THE
BESTSELLING O'MALLEY AND SWIFT
CRIME THRILLER SERIES!**

A holiday they'll never forget.

After the distress of Annie O'Malley's last case, she's
in need of a bit of rest and recuperation. So her sister,
Mim, books them on a flight to a luxury all inclusive
resort in Spain for a break.

But what was supposed to be a chance to sip sangria
and reconnect with each other after so long apart soon
turns into something terrifying when a group of armed
men storm the hotel and take the guests hostage.

With the help of Swift and the team back in Norfolk, can Annie and Mim find an escape route out of the resort and get themselves and the rest of the guests to safety?

Or will the holiday of a lifetime that was supposed to reunite the estranged sisters leave them torn apart forever?

Perfect for fans of LJ Ross, Alex Smith, Elly Griffiths, and Rachel McLean. O'Malley and Swift return in a thrilling instalment that will keep you hooked from the first page.

Buy at
www.ktgallowaybooks.com

THANK YOU!

Thank you so much for reading Deadly Games. It's hard for me to put into words how much I appreciate my readers. If you enjoyed Deadly Games, I would greatly appreciate it if you took the time to review on your favourite platform

You can also find me at www.KTGallowaybooks.com

ALSO BY K.T. GALLOWAY

Click through the covers for store links

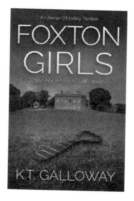

An Annie O'Malley Thriller

WE
ALL
FALL
DOWN

Ring a ring o' roses

K.T. GALLOWAY

An O'Malley & Swift Thriller

THE
HOUSE
OF
SECRETS

K.T. GALLOWAY

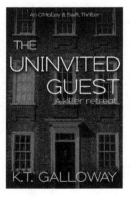

An O'Malley & Swift Thriller

THE
UNINVITED
GUEST

A killer retreat

K.T. GALLOWAY

An O'Malley & Swift Thriller

ONE
LAST
BREATH

K.T. GALLOWAY

Printed in Great Britain
by Amazon